'Christopher Hope was born in Johannesburg and writes about South Africa with inside knowledge and the wry, detached eye of a natural observer. *The Love Songs of Nathan J. Swirsky* is a short, unshowy book yet it convincingly recreates the jumpy atmosphere of a society trembling on the brink of full-scale apartheid – of decent people sliding inexorably into an almost casual acceptance of intolerance and racial hatred'
Independent on Sunday

'Touching and amusing . . . These seemingly artless short stories are told without a wasted word'
Mail on Sunday

'*The Love Songs of Nathan J. Swirsky* is a welcome comic performance . . . It is a wonderfully warm, natural and evocative portrait of small-town life, written with the vivid exactness of childhood memory and engaging good humour'
Irish Times

'These stories are brilliantly constructed and paced, individually warm and collectively superb'
Herald

'One of the funniest books around'
Woman's Journal

'A deft, funny and subtly gruesome book . . . By hints, omissions, throwaway remarks the nostalgic glow that bathes these stories is made dim and chilly. Racial tension, violence and murder shadow the sunlit comedy and turn it to laughter in the dark'
Time Out

'A whole world produced in simple strokes . . . life-size characters tumble from the page'
Literary Review

Christopher Hope was born in Johannesburg. He has published six novels: *A Separate Development* (winner of the 1981 David Higham Prize for Fiction); *Kruger's Alp* (winner of the 1985 Whitbread Prize for Fiction); *The Hottentot Room* (1986); *My Chocolate Redeemer* (1989); *Serenity House* (shortlisted for the 1992 Booker Prize); and *The Love Songs of Nathan J. Swirsky* (1993). He has written two works of non-fiction: *White Boy Running* (1988), which won the CNA Literary Award in South Africa, and *Moscow! Moscow!* (1990).

Also by Christopher Hope

FICTION
A SEPARATE DEVELOPMENT
LEARNING TO FLY AND OTHER TALES
KRUGER'S ALP
THE HOTTENTOT ROOM
BLACK SWAN
MY CHOCOLATE REDEEMER
SERENITY HOUSE

NON-FICTION
WHITE BOY RUNNING
MOSCOW! MOSCOW!

POETRY
CAPE DRIVES
IN THE COUNTRY OF THE BLACK PIG
ENGLISHMEN

FOR CHILDREN
THE KING, THE CAT AND THE FIDDLE
THE DRAGON WORE PINK

THE
LOVE SONGS
OF
NATHAN J.
SWIRSKY

CHRISTOPHER HOPE

PICADOR
IN ASSOCIATION WITH MACMILLAN LONDON

First published 1993 by Macmillan London Limited

This edition published 1994 by Picador
a division of Pan Macmillan Publishers Limited
Cavaye Place London SW10 9PG
and Basingstoke
in association with Macmillan London Limited

Associated companies throughout the world

ISBN 0 330 32329 6

'Nativity'
First broadcast in slightly different versions as 'Avante!' on 23 December 1991
and 'Relax!' on 24 December 1991 on BBC Radio 4, and first published in
The New Yorker, 28 December 1992/4 January 1993.

'Pink'
First broadcast on BBC Radio 3 in 1993.

'Precious'
First published as 'Strydom's Leper' in *Colours of a New Day* (Laurence Wishart, 1990).

'Arrivederci!'
Jointly published and broadcast in a different form as 'My Good Fairy' by the *Guardian* and
BBC Radio 3 on 23/24 February 1991 and subsequently as 'Arrivederci!' on BBC Radio 4,
25 December 1991. Anthologized in *Telling Stories*, 1992.

'Bravo!'
First broadcast in a different form on BBC Radio 4, 26 December 1991.

'Maundy'
First broadcast in a slightly different form as 'Warmer' and 'Maundy' on BBC Radio 4, 17/20
April 1992, and first published in *The New Yorker*, 1 June 1992. Anthologized in *Best Short
Stories*, 1993.

'Aloft!'
First broadcast in a different form on BBC Radio 4, 27 December 1991.

Lines from 'The Love Song of J. Alfred Prufrock' by T.S. Eliot are reproduced by kind
permission of Faber and Faber Ltd.

1 3 5 7 9 8 6 4 2

A CIP catalogue record for this book is available from
the British Library

Phototypeset by Intype, London
Printed and bound in Great Britain by
Cox & Wyman Ltd, Reading, Berkshire

IN MEMORY OF GRAHAM HARVEY
(1944–1992)
GENIAL SPIRIT . . .

I have heard the mermaids singing, each to each;
I do not think that they will sing to me.

The Love Song of J. Alfred Prufrock
T. S. ELIOT

CONTENTS

NATIVITY

NATHAN Swirsky came to Badminton just before Christmas of 1950. New houses rose raw on Victoria Road or William Street at the rate of one a month. The gardens our fathers fought so hard to establish were pretty poor affairs. Returning home from the desert war in Egypt and Libya, they began battling the bare veld. Every weekend they wrestled the hard, red earth into gardens.

Badminton was a new housing estate built outside Johannesburg for returning soldiers. Its streets were named after English kings and queens, because we were English South Africans. Behind the houses ran the sanitary lanes, where the night-soil men drove their horse and cart after dark and collected the black rubber buckets before we woke.

My friends Tony and Sally lived opposite me, in Henry Street. Next door to Tony and Sally lived Eric and Sammie. Their uncles were famous cricketers. Their ma, dark and panting, chased them in the garden, from time to time, trying to box their ears. Eric often ran away from home. To one side of us lived the Strydoms. Mr Strydom had not fought in the War because he was Afrikaans. On the other side lived Maggie. But she didn't really count because we hardly ever saw her. And when she showed off we weren't really supposed to look because usually she wasn't wearing any clothes. She ran round and round her house very fast

3

until her father caught her and threw a blanket over her.

Sometimes the water truck came and sprayed the streets to keep the dust down. Once a week, Mr Govender, the greengrocer, visited Badminton. And Errol, the man who sold topsoil for our gardens. But mostly nothing much happened. Until Swirsky came to live on the estate. Swirsky was made for trouble, my mother said.

The boxy new houses, with their corrugated-iron roofs, ran down a slope to a small stream and a copse of giant bluegums. Five years after the War ended soldiers, who had gone to fight against Germans, had turned into gardeners in uniform. My father worked in his Army boots. Gus Trupshaw wore a sailor's blue shirt. Maggie's father, in the garden next door to ours, wore his khaki puttees because, he said, they kept stones out of his shoes.

Our fathers looked up from their zinnias, mopped their brows, and said, 'It's hotter down South than it was up North, make no mistake.' 'Up North', they also called 'the Western Desert'. It was confusing. But our fathers never explained. They knew where they had been.

They cursed the African heat. They cursed the stubborn shale that had to be broken up with picks, forked over, sieved, spread and sweetened with rich brown earth, delivered by Errol the topsoil man.

They cursed the burglars. My mother said that there were swarms of burglars hiding among the bluegum trees. They ran down the sanitary lanes at night and slipped into the houses like greased lightning. As I lay in bed I saw the sanitary lanes teeming with burglars and night-soil men, coming and going.

Swirsky arrived wearing a most deadly moustache. The back window of his Opel Kapitän piled with bottles of blood-red mercurochrome and packets of *Joywear* Stretch Nylons in attractive shades of 'Bali Rose' and 'Jamaica Rum'. And he came from the direction of the dynamite factory. That I am sure of. Within what seemed about two minutes flat he had opened the doors of his pharmacy, built in the window a castle from green cough-drop boxes and hung above it a silver star on a length of fishing line.

'*Grüss' Gott*,' said Swirsky to Papas, who ran the Greek Tea Room at the end of the line of shops on Charles Drive which served the estate. The line was short: the Badminton Bottle Store; Swirsky's new pharmacy; Mr Benjamin, the Rug Doctor; and Papas, who sold everything from newspapers to pins. Everything except tea and cake.

'They say that all the time in Switzerland,' said Swirsky. 'It means God's greeting. I've just been abroad, as you can probably guess.'

'I was born abroad,' Papas said. 'Abroad is where I began.'

Swirsky was English. Or so he said. My mother didn't believe him. 'English or Jewish?' she said. 'He can't have it both ways.'

Within a week Swirsky had lettered 'A Merry X-Mas to All My Customers' in shaving cream soap along the length of his window, just above the green turrets of his cough-drop castle and just below the silver star on the fishing line. The heat of December would dry out the shaving cream and he would replace his Christmas message each day. With my friend Sally, from across the road, I liked to watch him. Sally and I would kneel on the pavement and rest our elbows on the ledge of Swirsky's window. We called it 'going to see the show'. Sally said it was better than going to the bioscope in Orange Grove. I agreed even though I had never been to the bioscope – just because Sally said it so nicely, and smiled.

At three in the afternoon Swirsky would lift his white coat, like a skirt, and climb into the window, lather up the shaving mug he carried and write the message again, his tongue between his teeth.

'I have to letter it the wrong way round.' He waved his

shaving brush. 'Leonardo da Vinci did something like this. *Avanti!*'

Swirsky was soft and pink. His black hair was combed in a centre parting and his eyes were the colour of the blackest olives. He smelt of liquorice and Will's Gold Flake Cigarettes.

This rather amused Gus Trupshaw. 'Gold Flake is the man's cigarette that women like,' he said to my father as they sat in the ex-servicemen's club in the corner of the kindergarten hall. I sat under a plastic palm tree, sipping lemonade.

'I've never understood what women like,' said my father.

'You're missing the point, Gordon,' said Gus Trupshaw.

My father breathed out hard. 'I see what you mean!'

'What does he mean?' I asked.

'Little pitchers have big ears,' Gus Trupshaw said.

'If I told you your mother would murder me,' my father looked at me. 'Let's not break up the happy home, shall we?'

Swirsky's white chemist coats were the loveliest ever seen. He washed, starched and ironed them himself. They were wafer thin, each thread frozen, so crisp you heard him crackle.

'How that man manages without a servant, I cannot imagine,' said my mother. 'Of course, I suppose if you travel as much as he does, a servant is just too much bother. Like keeping a cat. What do you do with it when you head for the bright lights?'

Swirsky's moustache was black, sharp, shiny. It was honed to a razor's edge, jet fighter's wings beneath his nose. Sally liked it so much she copied it in black eyebrow liner she got from her mum's sample case, and she rolled down the grass bank in her garden shouting '*Avanti! Avanti!*' until her brother Tony went and blabbed, and Sally's mum made her take it off.

'Have a little respect, my girl. I happen to represent that line in cosmetics myself,' she said and drove off in her light blue Austin A40.

'You are such a total drip!' Sally told her brother. She turned her wide blue eyes to me. 'Let's go and look in Swirsky's window, Mart. But we won't take him.'

Tony followed about ten steps behind us all the way to Swirsky's chemist shop and every now and then Sally said, 'I think there must be something following us, Mart. I can smell something.'

Tony said, 'Well, it's a free country. I can walk wherever I want.'

Eric came by from next door with his little brother Sammie. Sammie knew so much. He was little and dark with big brown glasses on the end of his nose and he could throw a clay ball faster and harder than anyone else when we had fights down by the river bank using long whips of willow to launch them. Sammie could knock you down if he hit you plumb centre. Eric was whistling 'The Railroad runs through the middle of the house...' Sammie said, 'Did you know that when the King and Queen came to South Africa a few years ago, the King made this lady-in-waiting swim out to sea and pretend to be drowning just so that he could watch the lifeguards rescue her?'

'Rubbish,' said Sally, 'the King would never do that.'

But Sammie went right on. 'Swimming close by her was a certain major and he really thought she was drowning so he rescued her first. Then she told him that it was all a joke.'

'Don't tell lies,' Sally said, very shocked.

'I believe you,' called Tony from way behind us.

'Why is Tony walking behind us?' Eric asked.

'Who?' said Sally and looked around, shaking her head. 'I don't see anyone. Close the door behind you, Mart. Just in case.'

Swirsky was in his shop window on his hands and knees pitching a small tent, midway between a pyramid of aspirins and a tree made entirely of boxes of laxatives called 'California Syrup of Figs'.

'I'm trying to build a nativity scene. It's not really my line of country. But I must tell you that I have visited the original – when I was in Israel. Bethlehem's a lovely little town. I can recommend it, when you're next down that way.'

A crowd of black servants watched from the other side of the glass. Swirsky lathered up his shaving mug and painted his Christmas greeting on the window. 'Leonardo da Swirsky!' The servants clapped. Tony watched him through the window, pressing his lips to the glass. They looked like the undersides of two pink snails.

We built quite a good manger. Though we didn't have straw, we found a pile of sawdust in a shipment of German thermometers and used that. Sammie and Eric fetched their lead farmyard animals. Sally offered a doll named Antoinette and an old cradle that had belonged to her Dutch great-grandmother.

'Just wait till Mom finds out you've taken her yellow-wood cradle,' Tony shouted from the other side of the glass. And Sally said to me, 'Did you hear something wet, Martin, something with blobby, drippy lips?'

Sammie cut three kings from cardboard and coloured them in wax crayons.

'Why is one of the kings black?' Swirsky asked. And when we told him he said, 'Fancy that. So there was a black chappy in on all this?'

I offered a statue of Our Lady of Perpetual Succour which had stood out in the garage next to the crate of Trotter's jellies. And for the figure of Joseph we used a large wooden puppet of Sinbad the Sailor got from the props room down at the kindergarten hall.

8

'Isn't this a lot of fun?' Swirsky said as he fitted a blue light bulb to the tent pole holding up our manger. 'There's more to this nativity business than meets the eye.'

Swirsky's nativity made people talk all over Badminton. My mother said, 'I'm afraid this is rather typical. They're taking over.'

'Who are taking over, Monica?' my father wanted to know.

'Did you know, Gordon,' my mother demanded, 'that Martin has gone and given Mr Swirsky the statue of Mary for his window? And there is a great crowd of servants dressed to the nines outside that window day and night. When Margot van Reen and I went to the tea room today we had to step off the pavement and walk round them. If this goes on I foresee ugly scenes by Boxing Day. Mark my words.'

'Putting a Christmas crib in your shop window is not against the law. At least not yet. But who knows? Judging by the way this bunch of fascists who run this country are carrying on, it might be illegal soon.'

'It's not a Christmas message. It's "X-mas", according to Mr Swirsky, if you please,' my mother said. 'And I'd be very grateful if you didn't use that word. All over the estate children are calling each other fascists. It's not a word for eight-year-olds. If you're not careful, the servants will be using it next.'

Swirsky offered to take us to the Christmas grotto in the Cape To Cairo Department Store. My mother said I could go, providing that I did not speak to strangers. Eric and Sammie couldn't come because their ma said she wasn't sending her boys shopping with a stranger. Sammie told her the Christmas Lucky Dips were free, but she said that nothing in life was free. And then she made her boys take back their lead farmyard animals from Swirsky's window.

'I'm really sorry, Mr Swirsky,' Eric said. 'But our ma says that we have to.'

'Never mind, boykies,' Swirsky said, 'the loss of a couple of moo-cows won't kill my nativity.'

Sally, Tony and I drove to the grotto in Swirsky's Opel.

'Remember, Martin,' my mother told me before we left, 'if you get lost, stay exactly where you are.'

Down in the Christmas grotto, Santa Claus sat on a red throne bright with silver glitter. Beside him was a reindeer with one big yellow glass eye and horns. It was pulling a sleigh piled with cardboard boxes tied with ribbon. The grotto was very warm and full of kids holding their mothers' hands. The cardboard boxes in the sleigh were tied up in big ribbons, pink for girls, blue for boys. A sign said: *Strictly one dip only per child.*

'It looks like a moose,' said Sally. 'Not a reindeer.'

'You've never seen a moose,' her brother said.

'If you kids don't simmer down, you can forget about Christmas,' a man suddenly said in a rough voice. 'And remember, only one dip each.'

Father Christmas wore a big cottonwool beard and his lips were pink. His hood hung over his eyes. 'OK, boys and girls. Who's first?' Several children began crying.

Tony went first and came back swinging his lucky dip. Swirsky pushed me forward. I looked at Father Christmas' cottonwool eyebrows. Where his robe ended he showed grey flannels and black shoes. His lips were not only pink, they were wet and I didn't like to look at them. At least boys could whisper in his ear. Girls had to sit in his lap and he had this way of spreading his legs so they fell into the red gap between them. I told him I wanted a box-cart for Christmas. He told me I would have to be very good. I never imagined for a moment I would ever get a box cart but what was the point of asking for something you knew you wouldn't get if you didn't go all the way? Papas made them – wooden crates mounted on four pram wheels, and steering shafts wrestled into shape from wire coat hangers. I saw the steep rise at the top of Henry Street and heard the wind in my ears.

Swirsky pushed Sally forward. Tony whispered to her, 'He smells of beer.' Sally made as if to go forward and then she put her chin on her chest and began fiddling with the red bow at her waist. Her toes pointed inwards and the more Swirsky pushed her forward the more her toes pointed inwards. Swirsky left her then and walked over and whispered in the ear of Father Christmas who wiped sweat from his brow and shook his head. He lifted his woollen eyebrows to the queue. 'Next please,' said Father Christmas.

'Sorry squire, I'm not going till I get the box,' said Swirsky.

'I never knew people like you believed in Christmas,' said the man in red.

'I don't believe in you,' Swirsky said loudly.

Father Christmas stood up. He was a big man. 'Is that so?' he said. And he reached up and with a loud tearing sound he ripped off his beard. There were a lot of people crying now.

'I hope you're really pleased with yourself,' Tony whispered to his sister.

The manageress arrived and made Father Christmas put his beard back. Then she gave Swirsky a lucky dip and she led us quickly out of the grotto.

On the way home we sang 'Hold Him Down You Zulu Warrior' and Swirsky advised us to travel to Rhodesia whenever possible. It was the coming country, he said. He recommended the Leopard Rock Motel. 'Baths in every room and billiards. You look like a billiard player to me,' he said to Sally who sat beside him saying nothing and holding her lucky dip to her chest.

Inside the lucky dips there were six marbles in a canvas bag, a spinning top painted with colours of the rainbow, a cardboard kaleidoscope, three balloons and a rubber dagger, if you were a boy, and a face mirror for girls.

Back in Badminton we found the crowds had gone from Swirsky's nativity. Instead there was a great hole in the window and a lot of glass on the pavement. And there was a brick inside the window. The pup tent had collapsed on the crib. The blue light was still on. The three kings were buried but they were OK and the yellow-wood cradle had tipped over. We helped Swirsky clear the window. The only thing missing was Sally's doll Antoinette, the Christ child.

Mr Swirsky looked at his broken window. 'Well, that wasn't much of a nativity,' he said. 'But it was fun, while it lasted.'

He went over to Papas' place because he had a brother in Orange Grove who ran a used-car lot and he got from him a big wooden crate and boarded up his window until after Christmas. When he'd finished his window read: *N. Rubin and Partners, Potato, Onion and Poultry Suppliers. Racehorse Feed Specialists, Ship's Chandlers.*

'My godfathers!' my mother said. 'I don't know which looked worse. The crib or the boards.'

Gus Trupshaw said that people should keep out of other people's religions. 'Tigers don't mate with bears, do they?'

'Excuse me,' said my mother, 'there was nothing religious about Swirsky's window. Of that we can all be quite sure. As if Christmas wasn't difficult enough. On Christmas Eve all the servants will be drunk. On Boxing Day they'll be round for their Christmas boxes and before you know it, they'll be banging on the street poles and shouting "Happy! Happy!" And then the New

Year will be on us. Where will it end, I ask? Where will it end?'

'I'm sorry about your dolly,' said Swirsky to Sally. 'I'll get you another.'

'It's all right,' said Sally. 'I hate dolls, really.'

DRAGONS

O N Christmas morning we went to Uncle Monty's Pleasure Farm for a picnic lunch. And because my father said we couldn't really leave him behind, we invited Swirsky along.

My mother warned me not to wish him a happy Christmas. 'The polite way of greeting a person like Mr Swirsky on Christmas morning is to say – "Have a happy holiday".'

We travelled in convoy. My father led the way in his new pale green Vauxhall, with my mother saying, 'Martin, do try *not* to breathe on the windows, it obstructs your father's vision.' And my father rolling down his window whenever someone overtook us and waving his fist at them and shouting, 'Bloody cowboys!' He only ever took the car out on Sundays and holidays though he spent his evenings cleaning it, polishing the seats and patting the bonnet.

'She's not a bad old bus,' he liked to say.

Gus Trupshaw followed in his truck and he wore an Hawaiian shirt with an orange sun climbing over a black palm tree. Eric's Ma and Pa sat up front in the cab, beside Gus Trupshaw, wearing their bowling outfits; brown shoes, cream shirts and sun hats with lettuce-green brims. Their ma was short, dark-faced and she had very broad shoulders and a voice rubbed raw by the cigarettes she smoked. Eric and Sammie rode in the back of the truck. Eric was trying to whistle

'Good Night Irene' against the wind. His little brother Sammie was wearing a pair of blue swimming flippers and reading a book about Rome. The brothers were always reading and this upset their Ma who used to snatch their books away and chase them into the garden. Sometimes she liked to chase them around the garden, swatting at them with the books she'd taken away. Servants passing in the street would stop to watch. 'Oh, no, madam!' they called out. But she didn't hear them. No one listened to servants.

Behind Gus Trupshaw came Sally and Tony in their blue Austin A40. Sally's Mom was tall and thin and always smelt good. Her husband had died in the war Up North and now she travelled in cosmetics. She was wearing the sunglasses she had bought from Swirsky for her trip to England.

Her plans for a visit 'home' had begun when Swirsky showed her an advertisement for the Union Castle line. 'It's the only way to go,' he said, 'if you're visiting the home country. Rest, relax, recuperate. That's the ticket.' The advertisement showed a ship's officer surrounded by four women in shorts. He wore a cap and had braid on his sleeves.

'He's showing the ladies his sextant. You'll have the time of your life,' Swirsky told Sally's mum when she had bought her ticket. He winked. 'The merry widow.'

And he whispered to my mother, 'A shipboard romance, perhaps?'

My mother said, 'Mr Swirsky!'

Swirsky laughed. 'It's a big wide world out there, Monica, believe me. And you never know what'll happen.'

'Some of us, who are not yet nine, would prefer not to know,' said my mother, flicking her eyes in our direction. 'Let's get Christmas over before we start talking of foreign romance.'

Swirsky brought up the rear in his new car. He'd sold the Opel soon after arriving in Badminton. And he'd bought a new

Ford. Before we set off he let all of us try the new press-button door opening; and he let our fathers try his new key-turn starter. He tried to get my mother to touch the upholstery but she said she was much more interested in getting to Uncle Monty's in time, thanks very much.

He wore a pair of loose khaki shorts, very tiny seal-grey ankle socks and open-toed sandals. His calves were white and meaty. His knees looked soft and blind. His black chest hair stuck through his white shirt.

'Guaranteed one hundred per cent pure bloody rayon,' Swirsky said and wiped sweat from his forehead. His hair was plastered across his head. Only his moustache was cool, looking perfect daggers under his nose.

My father set a slow pace and cars sped past. 'Bloody Don Fangio!' My father shook his fist.

'Just ignore them, Gordon,' said my mother. 'We want to get there in one piece.'

Uncle Monty's Pleasure Farm was a collection of dark tangled woods, a great, muddy swimming pool and stretches of hot yellow grass given over to camping, picnicking and caravaning. The thing to do was to get to the shelter of the trees before the heat struck at about eleven in the morning.

But because we were taking no chances ('We're taking no chances – this is Christmas!' my mother used to warn), we usually arrived at about nine when most of the rest of the country was still opening its presents. This meant opening ours at about seven in the morning and ordering the maids into the house at six o'clock. The servants always complained at the early hour of starting. People with large families might have as many as four servants, particularly those who had spent time in Nyasaland. For some reason, said my mother, 'ex-Nyasa people' were the worst.

They might have a cook, a housemaid, a nanny and one, or even two gardeners.

'Everywhere you turn there are domestics underfoot,' my mother liked to reflect. Remembering Nyasa families she had known, with their crowds of servants. 'It's like the last days of the Roman Empire.'

'Nyasaland is densely populated,' my father said.

'That's no excuse,' my mother said firmly.

We had only Nicodemus, who came with the house. So our Christmas mornings ended sooner than just about anyone else's. Servants sat across the room and were called to the tree when their turn came for presents. Nicodemus crossed the room on his knees, like a soft thunder, and fetched his present from my father who always said, 'Happy Christmas, Nicodemus. Now off you go – *Humbaghashle!*' And Nicodemus humbaghashled back across the room in another peal of soft thunder.

When we arrived at Uncle Monty's we settled under the bluegums squinting up through the big broad branches calculating that here we would have some shade at noon. The men got out the barbecue and the meat. The women took out buttered bread and orange juice. Gus Trupshaw fetched the large zinc tub for the beer which he kept in the back of his truck and he broke up a slab of ice he had collected from Papas at the Greek Tea Room. He worked with a hammer and chisel that he stored beneath the seat of his truck. This was the way the men kept their beer cold. It was a matter of the first importance, my father liked to say.

'I asked Papas if he wanted to join us,' said Trupshaw, 'but Papas said not.'

'The Greeks pay more attention to Easter than Christmas,' said Swirsky. 'It's their religion.'

'I suppose you should know,' said Gus Trupshaw.

And this was a signal for all of us to say, 'Have a happy holiday, Mr Swirsky!'

Swirsky settled back with a beer. 'This is the life – Happy Christmas, folks!'

It always got hotter. The fathers started the fire and it got hotter still. In the blue smoke from the wood fire ash flakes rose and fell in the sunlight slanting through the branches of the bluegums and the men's foreheads slowly turned pink. Eric's Pa and Ma unrolled the tartan rug and lay on either side of it like bookends to keep it from blowing away. Both round and short, they turned down the brims of their bowling hats against the glare and said they would be taking forty winks.

'Before lunch?' my father asked.

'Before and after.'

Everyone found this very funny.

My mother preferred a canvas camping stool. She had a horror of the busy red army ants that made lightning rushes at the avocado sandwiches, waving their big pincers. 'Well,' she kept saying as she unpacked sandwiches from their greaseproof wrappings, 'isn't this a change?'

The turkey drumsticks bulged inside their protective covering of silver paper. Accompanied by a tight twist of salt in blue paper the boiled eggs waited like bombs in the bottom of the basket. The men turned the meat on the barbecue. It began as sausage and steak and lamb chops but soon the heat and the smoke made it simply meat without a name. The sky was high and blue and the sun taller than anything. The meat had no name but it had a voice, which got so loud that the men cooking it raised their voices so as to be heard against its fatty muttering to itself. Every so often the fat spurted and Gus Trupshaw would suck his wrist and say, 'Damn, bugger!' And my mother would pause in her setting out of the picnic things and cough quietly and say, 'Excuse me!' She handed round ready mixed orange and water in enamel mugs with ears so big you had to take them in your fist. The men kept moving the zinc tub to every available piece of shade lest the sun melt the ice that cooled their beer.

By twelve o'clock there were crowds of people and those who arrived too late for the shade of the trees rigged tarpaulins from the sides of their cars and set out folding chairs and even pitched small tents. These were the experts. They came with their servants. Little black girls carried babies on their backs. Big black men made the fires. The smoke spread across the picnic ground and Swirsky called to the people next door who had arrived in an Opel Olympia with purple tinsel wrapped around its windscreen wipers, 'I say, can you keep your smoke down?' This amused the newcomers, a vast family of chunky grown-ups and shaven-haired, barefoot children with very brown legs. We could hear them calling to themselves, in a mock version of Swirsky's voice, 'I say, could you keep your smoke down, please?'

'Bloody swanks,' Gus Trupshaw said.

'Just ignore them,' said my mother. She unpeeled an egg very slowly and ate it carefully, staring stiffly into the sky. 'You might have thought that on Christmas day, at least, people would leave their servants at home. Can't we have one single day in peace?'

We ate our turkey and steak off paper plates. The forks had a way of snapping easily but the knives were serrated and so sharp they cut right through the paper and little bits of sand got mixed in the salad.

'I can hear your teeth crunching,' Tony said to Sally.

'So what? They're my teeth, aren't they?'

The men drank more beer. The women mostly sherry, except for Sally's mother who said, 'Make mine a Gee and Tee.'

We watched in fascination as Gus Trupshaw said, 'Coming right up, ma'am,' and poured her something which wasn't tea at all.

Gus Trupshaw said, 'I'll bet you're in training for your sea cruise, Lydia.'

And Sally's Mom banged him lightly on the chest with her fist and said, 'Oh, Gus – get on with you!'

We all pulled crackers after lunch. I got a red and black tin snapper in mine in the shape of a ladybird and swapped it with Sally for a plastic parachutist wearing a red plastic parachute. Eric and Sammie pulled their crackers together and fell over when the bangs came. Eric found a pair of dice in his. Sammie's cracker was empty.

'What a swiz!' said Sammie.

'The dice of death,' Eric said.

His mother sat bolt upright on the tartan rug where she'd been sleeping and said, 'I'll give you dice of death all right, young man! What sort of Christmas talk is that?' And she took after him the way you go after a bee that's spoiling your picnic – slapping him with her bowling hat.

Eric hopped from foot to foot crying, 'No, no, please Ma, no!'

It might have been nasty. Swirsky saved the day by reading out his riddle: 'Where can I go on holiday without leaving home?' Eric's ma stopped to think about it. Before anyone could answer he said, 'I'm going to Ru-man-ia!' Then he took us all swimming.

He wore a shiny yellow bathing costume, pulling tight over his belly button its silk cord. We were amazed to see how much dark fur covered his chest and shoulders and even appeared in patches on his back. We stood by the side of the great stretch of green and brown water that was Uncle Monty's Water Sports Arena and watched people having water fights.

'Who fancies the waterslide?' Swirsky asked. Sammie and Eric put up their hands.

'Give those men a medal,' said Swirsky.

The waterslide began on a platform high above the pool. You took hold of the ring and sailed down a long dark dripping rope into the water.

Swirsky said, 'In actual fact, I'm reminded of the Vic Falls. The greatest falls in the world. The savage splendour of untamed Africa. Don't miss it when you're next in Rhodesia.'

That was the thing with Swirsky. The world seemed just down the road when you listened to him. And Paris too. Or Bethlehem. Or Rhodesia. Rhodesia was his favourite. It was 'a coming little country'. To hear him speak of it, you felt you really might be there by next week.

Swirsky took Eric and Sammie up the ladder to the dripping wooden platform high above our heads. Then he made a little speech. 'These are my volunteers. But before I leave, let me recommend the Vic Falls Hotel. If you're up that way, mention my name to the manager. He'll see you right.'

Then he sailed down the rope with Eric and Sammie clinging to his thick strong body hair like baby monkeys. They rose to the surface splashing and waving. Swirsky was spitting water from his mouth in a solid silver curve. Then he swam over to us.

'Do you want to try?' he asked Sally. 'No? Never mind. Have I ever told you about the Dragons of Kommodo? In Malaysia? If ever you're down that way, promise me you won't miss them. They eat horses.'

'Even their hoofs?' Sally wrinkled up her nose.

'Nose to toes, girlie,' Swirsky said firmly. 'There is no stopping a Kommodo dragon.'

Tony got this sharp look. Under his hay-coloured hair his face looked like a steel blade. Sally had hay-coloured hair too. But her face never turned into an axe-head. Tony got what Sally called his 'smarty pants' look. He wanted to show us he understood Swirsky's ways because he suddenly told him that the calmest place in South Africa was Pretoria, actually.

24

Sally said, 'Actually, I'll bet you it isn't. How do you know?'

'Half the time the wind's so soft you can't measure it,' said Tony.

'Blow me down,' said Swirsky. And he laughed in that way he had. Pushing his teeth out over his lip and whistling while his shoulders shook and his head jigged up and down very fast. We didn't like the way Swirsky laughed but we liked him so much in every other way that we pretended he wasn't doing it. When he stopped shaking Swirsky said, 'Now let's go and find the grown-ups.'

'Must we?' Eric asked.

'Bless me, boy, don't you like your old folks?'

'Couldn't I come and live with you, Mr Swirsky?'

'Not before you've been to Malaysia.'

'I wish I were a dragon,' Eric said. 'I'd eat more than just horses.'

Sally got this shiver in her voice: 'What'll you eat?'

'Just you wait and see.' Eric got these blurry eyes. We could see he was trying not to cry.

Swirsky licked his finger and stuck it in the air. 'I don't know about Pretoria, but I'd say Uncle Monty's Pleasure Farm is pretty calm in the wind department. And anyway, what about Sammie? You don't want to live with me, do you, Sammie?'

'I wouldn't mind,' Sammie said.

'Please, Mr Swirsky,' said Eric again. And we all looked at our toes.

'You wouldn't want to live with an old pill-pusher like me,' Swirsky said, drying his finger on his chest hair. 'Listen, boykie – stay here and practise on the waterslide. If you're good enough, you could turn professional one day. And live in America.'

★

When we got back to our campsite, Sally's mother wasn't wearing her sunglasses any longer. Her face was white as ice and she was crying, a lot. Eric's mum and dad were on their feet, wide awake and not taking forty winks at all. Gus Trupshaw was carrying his hammer and chisel. He gave the chisel to my father.

'You kids run off and play,' my mother ordered.

Gus Trupshaw gave the hammer to Swirsky. Then he ran to his truck and came back carrying his starting pistol. 'I vote we go and find the bugger!' we heard him say.

'I can't believe it,' my mother said. 'All you ask is a quiet day out – and this is what happens!'

We went and sat on the grass a little way away where we could hear clearly. My mother had her arm around Sally's mother and she kept saying, 'My godfathers!' Sally's mother had been for a stroll somewhere among the trees, beyond the camping area. She'd seen something. Or someone. She'd been frightened. She'd run away and lost her sunglasses. Swirsky asked her what she'd seen but she just shook her head and cried even harder.

Swirsky looked at the hammer in his hand as if he didn't know what to do with it.

'People who bring their servants on a picnic are asking for trouble,' said my mother.

Swirsky just stood there in his yellow bathing trunks, swinging the hammer. 'I don't think she was attacked,' he said, 'just a bit shaken.'

'Just a bit shaken!' my mother barked. 'On Christmas Day!'

Then Eric appeared, he was limping badly and there was blood all over his right foot. 'I just stood on a nail,' he said, 'a very rusty one.'

'I'll give you rusty nails!' his mother made a grab at him and Eric hopped away, pouring blood.

Swirsky stepped in then. Still wearing his yellow bathing

costume, and pulling his rayon shirt over his thick black hair, he gathered up Sally's mum still crying and Eric bleeding and saying, 'I think I might get lockjaw.' He packed them into his Ford and drove them back to Badminton, back to his shop, back to his shelves stacked with baby foods and bicarb and liver pills.

They talked about it for days. Like a doctor he was, they said on the estate. As good as a doctor he is, our Swirsky, they said. A sedative for her and an anti-tetanus jab for the boy. It was as good as you'd get in Harley Street. When Swirsky came round a few days later to return the hammer Gus Trupshaw called him 'Doctor Swirsky'. Even my mother said he showed real presence of mind, for a man who did so much travelling.

On Boxing Day we got the news. The City Council had given permission for an Old Age Home to be built on the Estate. On the other side of the main road leading to the dynamite factory. Across the way from Swirsky's pharmacy.

'It takes one to know one,' said my mother.

'One what?' I asked.

But all she said was, 'Never mind, I think we've had quite enough damage for one Christmas, thank you very much.'

PINK

IREMEMBER when my mother found Nicodemus laughing in the kitchen. She called me because she said she needed a witness. Nicodemus was leaning on the sink holding a yellow teapot. He was smiling and shaking at the same time, but I didn't think he was laughing.

My mother was short and dark and her job was to worry. When she had nothing else to worry about she warned me of the dynamite factory down the road. If that exploded, she said, it would blow us all to smithereens.

My father was tall and thin. His job was to garden – when he wasn't at the office. I never knew exactly what it was he did at the office but he would say to me, 'Martin, promise me you'll never be a desk-wallah.' And then he'd put on his Army cap and walk into the garden, sighing.

'I beg your pardon, Nicodemus?' My mother stared at the ceiling, being horribly polite. 'Is this a private joke? Or may we all join in?'

When he didn't answer she went over and leaned against the bread-bin with her arms folded. The bread-bin was of egg-yellow enamel, and its curved creamy door ended in a weighted lip that somehow always made me swallow. Sally's legs, below her knees, gave me the same feeling when seen from the side. So did the water truck when it sprayed our sandy streets in Badminton on

Thursday afternoons. The whiskers it grew curved and dipped as it moved down the exact centre of the road, turning dust into mirrors where the water hit, sending everything swimming, wet and free. We ran barefoot behind the water truck, swallowing easily.

'Well, Martin,' my mother said, lifting her eyebrows in the direction of Nicodemus. 'Can you see the joke?'

I did not have an answer to the question. I did not have an answer to lots of the questions my mother and father asked me. They got the habit from the advertisements they read and they liked to pass on the questions. Did I know the difference between ordinary tyred tubes and Lifeguard Safety Tubes? Both went bang at 75 miles per hour, but only one of them saved your life. Did I think I could recognize which one it was?

Of course I couldn't. 'Which is the real Linda Darnell?' my father asked, holding up a spark-plug advertisement from the *Reader's Digest*. I looked at pictures of two women wearing matching diamond tiaras in their black hair and identical necklaces. Which was the famous motion picture star from Hollywood? And which was the fake from Bronxville, New York? I looked hard but I couldn't for the life of me tell.

I looked instead at the spark-plug with its bulky steel belly and its silver-tipped chesspiece head. I had found old spark-plugs down on the rubbish tip behind the Greek Tea Room from time to time, when Papas and his cousin from Orange Grove had been working on their old maroon Nash which they kept up on blocks in their garage. I would wander over the rubbish tip collecting spark-plugs the way people collected sea-shells. A spark-plug lay in the palm so beautifully. I wanted to do something with those spark-plugs. Perhaps I wanted to do something for them. I felt they were so lovely that they should be cherished for themselves alone. But the spark-plugs wouldn't have it. They knew they had

32

their uses. And they could only be used for what they were used for.

'Follow his eyes,' my mother whispered, 'that's what I usually do. Africans are at the mercy of their eyes.'

I followed Nicodemus' eyes. He was looking through the window but there really wasn't much to see. Outside the fence Errol the topsoil man had parked his truck. It was an old Willys station wagon, with a bright toothy grille. Errol had cut off the roof to make his topsoil truck. He stood there with one leg on the side of his truck and he had rolled up his trousers and taken off the white shirt he usually wore. Errol's thin moustache shone when it caught the sun as he bent and dug deep into the dark brown topsoil in the back of his truck and threw it in a quick, perfect curve across the diamond mesh-wired fence to land in a growing, pointed hill exactly between my father's rather good Swan daisies and his fading Mexican sunflowers.

My father hated those sunflowers. Once I heard him telling Gus Trupshaw that the government had specially chosen Badminton as a new suburb for soldiers returning from the war because they knew the soil was so poor you'd have to slave your guts out to make so much as a sweet-pea bloom.

My mother watched Nicodemus half watching Errol spooning topsoil into our garden and shook her head. 'Heavens above! I hope we're not in for trouble. You know what they feel about Indians, don't you, Martin? Natives are at daggers drawn with Indians.'

Nicodemus and Errol looked like friends. I'd seen them playing drafts together on a wooden board, using bottle tops for counters. They called it 'clapboard'. Errol would slap his bottle tops down with all the force of a cap-gun going off. Nicodemus laughed and showed his long yellow teeth. Then he'd pull his naked black knees up to his chest, wrap his arms around them and whistle 'Whispering Grass' – the big Inkspots' number.

'All it takes is a spark,' said my mother. 'The Cato Manor Riots started from a single spark. An Indian boy was struck by a Black boy. Next thing, there were a hundred and fifty people dead and thousands in hospital. I only hope we're not in for something similar on our estate. That was only three years ago. I think I'll go and lie down. Keep watching his eyes, Martin.'

I watched Nicodemus' eyes like mad but they didn't really tell me anything. I watched as he made himself some porridge and poured golden syrup over it and went out to his room in the backyard. Then I leaned my arms on the bread-bin and watched Errol. When Errol had made his topsoil mountain he rested on his shovel standing in the back of his truck.

Then I saw the boy. He looked about fifteen, with a grey hat pulled down over his ears. He appeared from behind the truck, carrying a spade, and he used it to scrape up any loose soil that was lying about and add it to the pile. His job was to tidy up the topsoil mountain and pat it into shape. And I thought I knew then why Nicodemus had been laughing.

I went outside into the garden. Under his grey hat, in the shade of its brim, I could see the boy was very freckled. His wispy hair stuck out beneath the hat and he kept pushing it back under the brim. His skin, in the sunlight, looked not so much white, as pink. The back of his neck was red. The hair on his bare pink legs was white. He wore old maroon bedroom slippers with rainbow-coloured pom-poms on their toes. A thin black leather belt held up his long grey shorts. Only his shirt was new. I saw that straight away. His white shirt was Tootal guaranteed rayon. Those were the shirts Errol wore and Errol had sold six of them to Swirsky the chemist. Errol came around the side of his truck now, saw me and waved.

'This is Reggie. He's my boy.'

Errol's boy came over and shook my hand. I saw he had Errol's moist pink eyes.

'Don't ask him to speak,' said Errol. 'He can't. But he's got a good heart.'

My mother was at the kitchen window tapping loudly. She hissed something at me through the pane. As I turned to run indoors I could feel Errol and Reggie watching me.

My mother pressed her hand to her mouth. 'This is the giddy limit! I come into the kitchen for a glass of water and two aspirins and there he is. No wonder our friend found this amusing. It's all very well for him. He's not as dim as he likes to pretend, is our friend Nicodemus. You touched that boy, didn't you, Martin? Here, let me see.' And she took my hand and pushed open my fingers as if I held something secret.

'His name's Reggie. He's working for Errol,' I said.

My mother said, 'Just wait till your father hears about this. He'll give Errol Reggie all right.'

When my father got home from work she was waiting for him. She told him that Errol had a Reggie working for him. 'He touched Martin. I had to take him to the bathroom and wash his hand in Dettol. But I'm not sure Dettol will do it.'

My father shook his head the way he did when he found cut worms among his transplanted Scabiosa seedlings.

'What do you want me to do about it, Monica?'

'How should I know?' said my mother, 'That's up to you. You're the man. All I know is that something has to be done. We have children on this estate, don't we? I've never liked that Errol's face. Where does he get his topsoil from? How does he pay for that truck? You answer me that. And where did he find that creature?'

She took me to see Swirsky the chemist and asked if she should have used a stronger antiseptic. Swirsky said that it depended what she wanted to kill. My mother tightened her lips and said it wasn't killing she had in mind – but safety. Swirsky took my hand and examined each finger carefully and then said he thought I was quite safe.

My mother whispered that she had been reminded of the Cato Manor Riots. Swirsky smiled and said, that was ages ago. We'd put the riots behind us now. This was 1951. Time we moved ahead.

'I'll keep an eye open for Errol's little pink friend. I'm sure he's pretty harmless.' Swirsky gave me a yellow whistle and walked with us to the door of the shop. 'The whistle's made of glucose,' said Swirsky, 'and it looks and sounds just like a police whistle. If you blow it and the cops turn up, eat the evidence, Martin.'

'Please don't put ideas into his head,' said my mother. 'He has his nose stuck in a book for hours each day. I've told him he can't expect to see anything of the world with his nose stuck in a book.'

We stood on the pavement with Swirsky who looked so fine and cool in his perfect white coat. His moustache that day seemed rich and beautifully grown. When Swirsky pursed his upper lip his moustache rippled like a cornfield. He said he was thinking of taking a short holiday. Business had been good and a break always refreshed mind and body.

My mother said, 'I'm sure it's all very well for those who can shoot away, just as they please.'

'I'm thinking of Rhodesia,' said Swirsky. 'Now there's a country for you! The Leopard Rock Motel. Wireless in every room. Billiards. And a very good table.'

Across the road bulldozers were clearing trees. 'My goodness, what a mess. What on earth do they think they're doing?' my mother asked.

Swirsky put his hands into the pockets of his white coat. The coat was so tightly starched that his hands were outlined, finger by finger, in his pockets and his round stomach bulged gently. He rocked to and fro on his heels for a moment before he said: 'Surprised you haven't heard. That's the new Jewish Old Age Home.'

My mother sniffed. 'I'd heard, all right. But I couldn't believe my ears.'

When we got home my father was working at his roses, treating them for rust. He had made a hessian bag and tied it to a stick and planted the stick among his yellow Eclipse roses. He beat the bag with a desk ruler.

'Mind out,' he said to us, 'I'm giving my roses the Bordeaux powder treatment.'

'Gordon,' said my mother, 'this means *they*'ll be coming to Badminton in numbers.'

My father's ruler rattled on the bag raising clouds of powder and I began coughing.

'Martin,' said my mother calmly, 'do you mind? I'm speaking to your father.' She followed him into the rose bushes, waving away the cloud of powder. 'I've seen it myself, Gordon. It's on the main road to the dynamite factory. Right across the road from the shops. You can't miss it.'

My father stopped beating the hessian bag and cleaned his ruler on his shorts. 'What do you want me to do about it?'

'You can't do anything about it. *They*'re clearing the site. That's my point. It's too late, Gordon.'

'What have you got against homes, Monica?'

'I've got nothing against homes. *Per se.*'

'Well, that's all right then.' My father went back to beating the hessian bag.

I took out my whistle and blew it loudly.

'That's the spitting image of a police whistle, speaking sonically,' my father said. 'Be careful you don't have the boys in the black Marias down on us like a ton of bricks, Mart boy.'

My mother shook her head. 'I don't know what the world's coming to. We've already got the biggest dynamite factory in the southern hemisphere just a few miles down the road. And only yesterday I looked out of my own kitchen window and saw that Errol man up to no good you can be sure with a certain person who shall be nameless. And now we're loaded with a home for *them*.'

My father got down on his knees and stuck his head into the roses. He looked like a horse browsing in a hedge. 'Who told you?'

'Who else? *They* always know, don't they?'

'Know what, Monica?'

'You know what I mean. They look to each other, don't they? But ask about Martin's touching the you-know-whom, and they couldn't care two hoots. Swirsky took a quick look at Martin's hand and then talked about going on holiday. To Rhodesia, if you don't mind. Well, he's a bachelor. He can come and go as he likes. But I tell you I felt like saying to him – that's all very well for you, Nathan Swirsky. But some of us have to live here. We can't go popping off every two minutes to the Leopard Rock Motel. Some of us have to jolly well get on with it.'

I began eating my police whistle.

When Errol and Reggie began travelling together in Errol's truck, everything was very friendly. We traipsed behind them and Tony asked him how things were.

'Just lovely, my old china. First class.'

Reggie rode in the back of the truck sitting high on the pile of topsoil, next to the wheelbarrow they upended on the slopes of their topsoil mountain. Reggie's hatbrim lifted in the wind and he would pull it down over his ears so that it looked like some weird soup plate.

Reggie could not have been more than about fifteen. But Tony said that he was probably twenty-seven, at least.

Sally counted on her fingers. 'That's three times older than me.'

'Pink skins get older quickly,' Tony said. 'He has to keep out of the sun. That's why he wears a hat. His skin wrinkles fast.'

Sammie said, 'But I'm pink and I don't wrinkle.'

'You're white,' Tony said. 'Even if you look pink.'

Sally tucked her skirt into her pants and did a handstand. 'How do you know that?'

'Because if Sammie wasn't white he wouldn't be living in a proper house. He'd be out in the backyard in the servants' quarters.'

Sally walked on her hands, her blonde hair touching the ground. Her face was getting redder and redder. 'How do you know someone wouldn't let Sammie stay in their house? Even if he was pink?'

When we saw them together Reggie and Errol were a parade. Reggie would always wave at us from the pile of topsoil. They were a great team. Errol's truck drew up outside a house where topsoil had to be dropped and if they couldn't shovel it over the fence, then they'd pull the wheelbarrow down and Errol would shovel in the soil and Reggie would push the stuff in the barrow. Sometimes he gave us rides on his return trips. And the little bits of soft chocolate loam left in the warm steel bed in the barrow got into the creases of our khaki shorts and between our toes. We sat with our legs wrapped round each other and Reggie would bounce from foot to foot in his old carpet slippers and Sally said that it was just like riding in a rickshaw.

When he saw us Errol would pretend to be mad and begin shouting at Reggie, 'What are you doing, man? You messing about, hmm?' But he was smiling all the time and showing the gold in his teeth.

Then, one day, Reggie turned up wearing sunglasses. He looked really strange. As if he was on his way to a fancy-dress party, riding right up there on top of the pile while Errol drove slowly down Henry Street.

Lots of people came out to see him pass and Nicodemus began smiling again. It was as if he couldn't stop smiling and I followed him when he went outside to his room. Nicodemus lay on his bed and looked at himself in the scrap of mirror he'd hung from a nail above his bed. First he closed one eye, and then the other. He lay stretched on the bed in his white calico uniform with the scarlet piping around the collar and around the ends of his big, square shorts. When I asked him what the matter was he giggled and hid his face in his hands.

When my mother saw Reggie riding on the topsoil wearing his sunglasses she said, 'Who on earth does he think he is? King Farouk?'

Errol told us the glasses had been a gift, 'from Boss Swirsky'.

Sammie said he'd looked it up in a book. Pink people had very weak eyes. Sally said she'd seen Reggie lift his hat and his hair was white. Then Sammie said pink people had weak eyes and white hair. Sally said that was all rubbish and we should ask somebody who really knew about these things.

So we went up to the pharmacy but Swirsky wasn't there. He had pulled down the blinds in his window and there was a notice on the door in red ink:

Bi-annual vacation. To all my customers – Nathan J. Swirsky announces that he is taking a fortnight's well earned rest in Rhodesia. All emergency enquiries: Goldstone's Pharmacy, Cyrildene.

My mother asked my father to phone Rhodesia. 'I'm sure

Mr Swirsky will be keen to know about the chaos he's left behind. Tell him about King Farouk.'

My father said, 'He's probably out all day.'

'Leave a message, then.'

'A fat lot of good that will do! Imagine me saying to the manager – look old man, there's an albino bloke riding around in a topsoil truck on our estate. And he's wearing a pair of sunglasses given to him by Nathan J. Swirsky who is a guest of yours. Please tell Mr Swirsky that we have a bone to pick with him. Oh, and while you're at it, tell him that the Jewish Old Age Home they're building across the road from his pharmacy has already climbed three storeys. Tell him we know he's behind it.'

'I never said he was behind it.' My mother stared at her nails. 'I simply said he had more than an inkling of what was going on. My godfathers! The servants have probably known for weeks. They've got a nose for these things.'

My father pulled on his Army cap. 'What things?'

My mother said nothing till he gave up waiting for an answer and went into the garden. 'Now we know why Nicodemus was laughing in the kitchen.' She touched her finger to her lips. 'Don't we, Martin?'

BUNNIES

GUS Trupshaw had always been pretty cross about Errol's topsoil business. Now that Errol had Reggie he took to hooting whenever he saw them and yelling: 'D'you get a road-worthy for that old crock?'

Gus Trupshaw pulled up outside our fence one day when my father was ripping out a bed of beardless irises that hadn't taken. Trupshaw rolled down the window of his old Ford pick-up. He rubbed his bushy ginger eyebrows. He said: 'Hell, Gordon, that's not a truck he drives. It's a sawn-off jeep.'

'When Errol teamed up with Reggie,' Gus Trupshaw said to my mother, 'take it from me, Monica, I said to myself – that's not a partner, that's a personal liability.'

Errol must have taken it to heart. Because one day he turned up in a shining new vehicle. Reggie sat high on the hill of soil. People came out of their houses and watched the parade moving slowly down Henry Street. Reggie must have thought they were all pleased to see him because he smiled and waved to them. We climbed all over the new vehicle breathing in its perfumes of seat-leather and duco. Errol had pasted the advertisement from the *Reader's Digest* in the window of his cab. 'International! The finest all-purpose light truck ever!'

Gus Trupshaw came around a few days later to find out why my father was having trouble with his narcissi. He said: 'Your Indian's a shifty character.'

45

'Give me a native,' said my father, 'any time.'

'Give me neither. But if I had to choose, I'd also take a native. Every time.'

'You know where you are with a native,' said my father.

'You do, Gordon. You do.'

My father waved his hands sadly in the flowers. 'What do you think has blitzed these palookas of mine?'

Gus Trupshaw knelt on the lawn and took one of the big yellow trumpets between his thumb and forefinger. 'That's eel-worm. The little buggers are too small to see. But the blisters give them away. Where your narcissus is concerned, eel-worm is public enemy number one.'

When Errol got his new truck our fathers began complaining about his high prices. 'If I'm going to be robbed,' said Gus Trup-shaw, 'I can always ask the burglars down in the bluegums to do the necessary. I won't be taken for a ride by a slippery Bengali.'

Errol didn't care. 'No way will I drop prices, man. This is first-class loam.'

Reggie sat on top of the pile and gave everybody V for Victory salutes as the red truck trundled around the Estate. But he lived behind his sunglasses, where his weak pink eyes were hidden. Reggie really didn't see anything. And Errol, who was usually so sharp, didn't see what was happening in Badminton. Didn't feel how the air was getting thick. Didn't notice that Nicodemus wouldn't play clapboard with him any more.

'You can understand why natives had a go at coolies in the Cato Manor Riots,' said my father.

'Don't mention it,' my mother begged, 'it only takes a single spark.'

★

46

Then the storms came. The sky was a huge black wall. Splashes of lightning ran down the wall like milk. When the thunder clapped I put my fingers in my ears and my head sang. This is how it would be, I knew, when the dynamite factory exploded and blew us all to smithereens. Raindrops drummed on the red dust of Badminton. Our fathers went out into their gardens with umbrellas and shovels and tried to channel the water away from their flowerbeds. My father lost half his rockery. The floods tore precious blooms from their beds and washed them against the front fences of our gardens. My father's Mexican sunflowers broke free and floated off.

'Bloody no-good dago Johnnies!' My father put his hands in his pockets and walked around the garden kicking the dahlias.

My mother said, 'Gordon, please! There are little ears out on stalks!'

Gus Trupshaw said that Indians were always able to read the weather signs. All over Badminton Errol's topsoil washed away and flowed down the storm water drains in Henry Street and William Street and Alexandra Road and ended up again in the river which ran beside the bluegums on the other side of Edward Avenue. From there Errol had only to gather it up again to sell the same topsoil twice over.

'He should learn to play by the rules,' said Gus Trupshaw, 'or he can go back to Durban.'

'Or Calcutta,' said my father.

Our fathers called a secret meeting of the Torch Commando. About twenty-five ex-soldiers who hated the government. Usually the Torch Commando ran through the Estate after dark plastering letterboxes with their paper stickers, a fiery torch that appeared to be growing out of an ice-cream cone. The Torch Commando was supposed to fight the government because the government was a lot of dyed-in-the-wool fascists who had spent the War knitting socks for Hitler. When the 'Torchies' had been busy people got up in the mornings, looked at the stickers on their letterboxes, and pretended to be mystified.

Now the Torch Commando was fighting a war against Errol the topsoil man. They held a meeting in our kitchen and everyone on the Estate knew about it but no one said so because it was a secret. Gus Trupshaw came of course and Mr Strydom from next door and Eric's and Sammie's uncles, who played first-league cricket. Their father couldn't come because he had a Lodge meeting. And when we asked Sammie what a Lodge meeting was, he said he knew but his ma would kill him if he said. Papas from the Greek Tea Room was there, too, even though he was foreign and hadn't fought in the War.

My mother made cheese bites and polony sandwiches and carried them through to the dining-room where the Commando sat around the table. But she refused pointblank to use the password which Gus Trupshaw had suggested. 'I'm not going to say "eel-worms" every time I walk into my own dining-room. I know who I am.'

Gus said, 'Yes, Monica, but how do we know who you are?'

'I'll tell you who I am,' said my mother, 'I'm the one who makes the sandwiches.'

In the end it was agreed that she wouldn't have to say the password. She would just rattle the beer bottles before opening the dining-room door.

Everybody in Badminton said it had been a very good secret meeting. Papas had told them about his cousin in Orange Grove who had a contact in the gardening business. Each Friday Gus Trupshaw would drive out past Uncle Monty's Pleasure Farm and collect a load of topsoil. At the weekend, he would cover the Estate and then our fathers would buy from him and only from him.

It worked for a while. Gus Trupshaw's truck, loaded with topsoil, made its way down Henry Street on Saturday afternoons, leaking a little soil from its tailgate and listing awkwardly to the right. Because of the heavy rains there was thick black mud in Edward Avenue and twice the Ford got bogged down and our fathers had to push it out, with my father yelling, 'One, two, three, heave-ho!' with the back wheels spinning wildly and spraying their trousers with mud. Papas fell over and all the men cheered. Then they went down to the ex-servicemen's club in the kindergarten hall and drank beer.

'Honestly,' said my mother, 'aren't men the giddy limit? Promise me, Martin, that you'll never grow up to be as silly as that!'

Errol the topsoil man still didn't seem to care. He would drive down Henry Street and when he saw Tony, Sally, Eric, Sammie and me sitting out on the front lawn he would lift a thumb and show us a flash of his gold teeth. Because there was no work he sometimes let Reggie off outside Sally's house and went and parked down by the bluegums and smoked a cigarette.

Reggie would sit on the pavement with us, his knees pulled up to his chest, smiling a lot. Then, one day, Eric gave him a spinning top and taught him how to throw it. Sally showed him how she could walk on her hands. Reggie let us try his sunglasses, covering his eyes from the glare.

Tony asked him, 'Does it hurt when the sunshine touches you?'

'You don't have to shout so loud,' said Sally. 'Reggie can't speak. But that doesn't mean that he's deaf.' Then she stood on her hands and walked into my garden and Reggie followed her.

She said we should teach Reggie how to roll down the grass banks where the lawn sloped from the rockery, which the floods had half carried away. When Tony said it wasn't allowed, his sister said, 'This is Martin's garden and if he says we can roll down his grass bank, then we can. Can't we, Mart?'

Then Sammie arrived and before I could say yes or no Sally said to them, 'Martin says we can.'

'Your pants show when you do that,' said her brother.

'So what? They're my pants, aren't they?'

Sally took Reggie's hand and pulled him to the top of the bank. Then, speaking very slowly, and showing him with her hands what she meant, tucking her elbows into her sides and keeping her ankles tight together, she lay on the top of the grass bank and rolled quickly to the bottom.

Reggie took off his hat. He took off his slippers with the pom-poms. Last of all he took off his sunglasses and blinked at us, wetly. Looking at his moist eyes made mine water. He put his glasses inside a slipper. He covered the slippers with his hat. He lay down, on the top of the bank, and then sat up and gave the V for Victory sign. Then he lay down again and rolled down the bank.

Soon we were all doing it. We couldn't get out of the way fast enough when the next roller came down the bank and we would bump into each other at the bottom. We had forgotten about everything when a shadow fell on us.

'My godfathers!' my mother yelled. 'I turn my back for two minutes and this is what I find. One look at Nicodemus' eyes and I knew you were up to something.'

My mother's dark head to the side of the sun looked like a black moon. I tried to get up but the earth kept turning under me.

'I told you not to touch him, Martin. And what do I find? You're making bodily contact.'

She ran off to the garden tap and turned it on. She picked up the hosepipe. By now we were all standing up. Tony hopped from one leg to the other, holding the front of his shorts. He was crying. 'I told them not to. But they wouldn't listen.'

My mother was fighting the hosepipe nozzle as she ran towards us spraying water into the air. It made a rainbow. 'Shoo!' she shouted at Reggie. 'Shoo, shoo, shoo!'

Reggie stood up and grabbed his hat, glasses and slippers. Water from the hose hit his chest. His freckles showed through the white nylon shirt. When he turned water soaked his back. He was giddy like the rest of us because he dropped his glasses and hadn't time to pick them up again. Water streamed from his pants as he made for the gate. His bare feet left wet prints in the red dust as he ran down Henry Street. I stuck his glasses down my shirt front.

I was sent to my room every afternoon for a week. If I so much as showed my nose, my father said he would thrash me within an inch of my life. My mother said, 'I'm ashamed of you, Martin. I truly am.'

I put on Reggie's glasses and looked at myself in the mirror. All the world went dark.

From time to time I'd see Errol passing in his truck. But there was no sign of Reggie. One day Errol stopped outside my house at about five. My father was planting out some red mountain spinach which grows well in poor ground.

'What have you done with my boy?' Errol asked. 'Tell me that, boss. He was playing with your boy and now he's lost.'

My father took off his old Army cap and scratched his head. 'You just keep little pink eyes to yourself. Or I'll have his guts for garters.'

'He had a good heart, boss,' said Errol. 'Now he's gone.'

I went to bed that night and dreamed of Reggie amongst the bluegums beside the little stream. He was wearing his hat and his slippers. He turned his pale face and blinked his watery eyes. He said: 'I've lost my sunglasses, Martin. Help me. I'll go blind.' Then he darted away among the trees and I ran after him. He did have a voice after all! It spoke a little above a whisper. Somewhere behind me I heard Errol calling 'Reggie, Reggie.' I ran even faster. I wanted to give him back his dark glasses. But my legs melted and I couldn't move. Errol's cries got closer and I woke up sweating.

Gus Trupshaw's topsoil business began to fail. Shovelling was the problem. Gus Trupshaw said he had a dickey back. Then he could deliver only at weekends, after he got home from work. So Papas began ordering topsoil from Errol again – he said he couldn't wait for Trupshaw to get home from the municipality. Eric and Sammie's Ma followed suit. Soon everyone was using Errol again. And his new red truck went past my house every afternoon.

Errol put up his prices again. When my father complained, he said, 'I'm on my own now, boss. I have to work twice as hard.'

Of Reggie there was no trace.

We all watched the Jewish Old Age Home climbing into the sky. Papas, of the Greek Tea Room, had seen the plans. It was going to rise to five storeys. It was going to be an absolute mansion.

'They always look after their own,' said my mother. 'They'll have everything that opens and closes. No expense spared. What did Mr Swirsky think when he handed out sunglasses to that pink creature?'

'We gave them a real fright,' said Gus Trupshaw. 'No mistake about that.'

'Wait till I see Nathan Swirsky. Is he going to get a piece of my mind.'

Gus Trupshaw said, 'Between you, me and the gatepost, the servants are saying that Master Errol and the pink creature were a bit dainty. If you follow me.'

My mother said that she didn't follow him.

'I'm talking of bunnies.'

'Did you ever get the impression that there was a touch of the nance about old Swirsky?' said my father.

Gus Trupshaw winked. 'Know what you mean, Gordon. Wouldn't surprise me.'

That night I dreamed I met Swirsky, Errol and Reggie down among the bluegums. They were all wearing white coats. For some reason they didn't seem to see me. Each of them had their hands on the others' shoulders, just like Sally, Sammie and me when we rode, once upon a time, in Reggie's wheelbarrow. Swirsky, Errol and Reggie got down on all fours and began hopping about amongst the trees. When I said, 'Hello,' they got a terrible fright, and hopped away as fast as they could. They had fluffy cottontails stuck to their backs. I wondered why I had never noticed that before. And I thought to myself, yes, Gus Trupshaw had been right. They were bunnies, after all.

I ran away early the next morning. I took a banana from the fruit dish and I leaned on the dresser where my mother had leaned when she watched Nicodemus laughing. The heavy yellow swollen lip of the bread-bin still made me hungry. I buttered two slices of bread. I put Reggie's sunglasses in my pocket. I knew why Nicodemus had been laughing. I walked down Henry Street as the sun was coming up. When I walked past the municipal dam the sun was quite high. Everything was further away than I thought and I didn't know where I was going. I wondered if Sally would marry Sammie one day. I remembered her legs and that made me hungry and so I sat down behind some trees and ate my banana.

Behind me in the distance I could hear the choir of the Black Church of Zion over at the municipal lake singing 'Michael Row The Boat Ashore'.

I don't know how many hours it took before I arrived at Orange Grove where I knew Papas had a cousin. The traffic was suddenly heavier. I sat down outside a chemist advertising TY Tonic Yeast Tablets. There were boxes of them built into a great pyramid. They cost four shillings a bottle. In the window was a picture of a man sitting at a desk with a pen in his hand. 'He doubled his capacity for work and pleasure.' I wondered if Swirsky was back from the Leopard Rock Motel and what piece of her mind my mother would give him. After sitting there for a while I ate my buttered bread. I felt thirsty. I wondered about the dynamite factory exploding and blowing us all to smithereens. Would all of Badminton shoot into the sky like fireworks and fall back to earth still in one piece? Or would it shatter like broken glass and rain down bits of me, Tony, Sally, Eric and Sammie, and Swirsky?

I was sitting there on the chemist's window-sill counting the laceholes in my shoes when Errol pulled up in his red truck. 'Well, bossy, where you off to? America?'

Errol drove home into Badminton nice and slowly. It all looked cool and calm below me. The building cranes dipped over the Jewish Old Age Home as we turned into the Estate. Passing Swirsky's pharmacy I noticed that his blind was up and I knew he was back from Rhodesia. We sailed down Henry Street and stopped outside my house.

My father came out: 'What are you doing up there, Martin?'

Errol said, 'You lost your boy, boss. I brought him back, for nothing.'

Errol lifted his hand to me, high on the pile of topsoil, on the back of his truck. Only the midday sun was higher. I hoped Sally and Tony were watching. Then I held up two of my fingers in a V for Victory.

Then through the kitchen window I saw Nicodemus. My mother was behind him and I guessed she was trying to follow his eyes. I reckoned I knew why. It was too dark to tell for sure through Reggie's sunglasses, but he seemed to be laughing.

PRECIOUS

TONY said, 'You can tell as soon as you look at him. Half his nose is off. And there are these patches all over him. Pink patches.' He said this before he ran indoors for about three hours.

His sister Sally watched him go: 'He'll be gone at least three hours. I can't stand it when he runs off to the lavatory just as I work out how to bowl him. Do you think this is a good grip, Martin? Do you think this is a googly?'

Her fingers curled around the tennis ball like little white snakes. Her legs were bare and she dug the toes of one foot into those of the other as though a part of her body was holding a distant conversation with another part. Her gingham skirt was tucked into her white bloomers.

'That's a leg-break.'

'It would have got him out. It would have smashed his wicket to hell and gone.'

High above us, against the sun in the hot white afternoon that turned her hair buttery, the hawks were hanging.

'How's this?'

'That's an off-break. A googly goes the opposite way.'

'He wouldn't have known the difference, would he? I'd have skittled him. So he runs and hides. He believes in hiding.'

Tony came back into the garden and picked up his bat. His

shorts were hoisted above his waist, almost as high as his chest.

'He can't be a leper. He doesn't have a bell. Lepers always carry bells,' Sally said.

'That was in the Middle Ages,' said Tony. 'This is 1951. You don't expect lepers to be carrying bells in 1951.'

Sally threw the ball down hard on to the lawn. 'I'm too hot to play.'

'You're a bad loser,' said her brother. 'Mart, bowl us a few balls.'

'I don't hide,' said Sally. 'At least I don't love hiding.'

Eric came by from next door. He was whistling 'The Tennessee Waltz' and trying to juggle three tennis balls.

Eric said, 'Can I play?'

'You can field,' Tony squinted at the hawks overhead. 'Mart's bowling.'

He was scared of Eric's talents. It ran in the family. Eric's elder brothers were both professionals, a batsman and a bowler. His old grandfather, who had died a few years before, had been an umpire. And his mother played a noisy game of pick-up sticks every Friday night on the green baize table in the dining-room. A pack of fifty Goldflake lay beside her always, like an open book. Her pick-up sticks fell into a coloured, jagged thistle and she went at them with broad yellow thumbs, denting the green baize. 'Ma's coming up from behind!' Eric said as she flipped her way through red and yellow. 'Ma's heading for black!' And she was. 'Ma's going to whip us,' yipped Eric. 'Shut up! Don't breathe on my sticks,' said his mother. And she whipped us.

'Tony's been hiding,' said Sally, 'in the lavatory. I'd have smashed his wicket to hell and gone. I had a googly ready!'

'When you've got to go, you've got to go.' Tony took up his guard and waggled his bat, looking around him like there were 10,000 spectators in the stands.

'I don't go when I've got to go,' said Sally.

'No, but you're perfect, aren't you? We can't all be perfection,' said her brother.

Eric dropped one of the tennis balls and it bounced down the sandy road hitting quartz pebbles and jumping about like it was drunk. Eric's ball went juddering down the hill and then spun left over the fence into Strydom's yard. That was just his luck.

'That's just my luck,' said Eric. 'Now Genghis will chew it to pieces.'

Almost everyone had dogs. With names like Nero and Tamburlaine. Genghis was black and ugly and about the size of a small horse and he half killed a dustbin man once. Genghis took the ball and kneaded it between his jaws.

'Why doesn't he just kill it?' Sally demanded, as we stood at the fence and watched, digging her toes ever deeper into the other set and screwing up her face. 'It's like he's trying to dissolve it in his spit.'

'Some snakes do that,' said Tony. 'Look – are we going to play or what?' He practised these really slinky late-cuts and drives and his cricket bat made this dry whirring sound in the hot air like birds' wings close to your ears. 'For God's sake, check that! Eric's going to feed himself to Genghis.'

Eric was leaning over the Strydoms' fence and trying to whisper Genghis closer to him, making kissing sounds. Clock, clock, went Eric's fingers softly.

That's when we saw him. He came out of a room in the back yard, well a shack more than a room really, and marched over to Genghis and began galloping in front of the dog. Every so often he'd try to whip the ball away but Genghis held on tight.

Tony danced up and down. 'I told you! Look at his nose. His nose is off, or bloody nearly. He looks like a leper.'

Sally said, 'But he can't be. Can he, Eric? Because lepers were from olden times, like in the Bible and that. We don't get them in, well, neighbourhoods.'

'Do you think just because you say that you don't get them in neighbourhoods, you don't get them? Because you've got another think coming,' Tony said.

'OK. So why would Mr Strydom want a leper then?' Her voice was high and quavery and carried over the fence. The leper's gallop got faster.

'Shut up, Sally,' I said.

'Shut up yourself, Mart.'

'Well, maybe they come cheap?' Eric spoke without taking his eyes off Genghis who had the ball tucked away in his cheek, like a kid chewing bubble gum. 'And old Strydom's really mean. Mean as night!'

There was just this one cloud in the sky, flat and spreading out in arms and legs. It looked like a dissected frog. The leper in the back yard was making little lunges at Genghis who seemed quite confused. Maybe the sight of this guy asking to be eaten put him off his food. The leper had a little shaved head and wide shoulders. He wore a pair of very long white shorts and a torn tunic with a square neck. The muscles on his skinny calves were black and stringy as a rope of onions.

Mrs Strydom came out into the yard, thin and angry. She waved her round pink face at us like an angry flower.

'Stop teasing the dog, Precious. He'll eat your head off otherwise. Do you hear what I say, you palooka?'

Precious stopped trying to get the ball but kept galloping on the spot, like he was pretending to be a pony. Genghis watched him, Eric's ball jammed between his jaws, dribbling a lot.

'Well?' said Mrs Strydom, looking over at us.

'Well,' said Eric, as if this was the start of a conversation and they were just about to have a bit of civilized chit-chat when actually everyone knew that Mrs S. was telling us to get lost.

'He's lost some of his nose,' Sally whispered.

'He's lost a bit of ear, too,' Tony pointed it out. 'See, the one on the right.'

'A lot of ear,' Sally murmured. 'It looks like what's left has been stuck on.'

'Maybe that's where it went,' I suggested, 'his nose and his ear. Bitten off. Probably by Genghis.'

'Or Genghis's aunt, sister or brother,' said Sally.

'The damage done to that boy was done by leprosy,' said Tony. 'Do you see his patches? That's the sign. Not the missing bits. Anyone can have missing bits. I saw these lepers in the Congo.'

'Last week?' his sister asked.

'In a book. With Dr Schweitzer. He has this hospital where he looks after them. In the Congo. You must know Dr Schweitzer.'

'Not if you know him,' Sally said. 'If you know him you'll keep him to yourself.'

'If you're waiting for the ball, then you're crazy if you ask me,' said Mrs Strydom to Eric. 'The dog's gobbed it to death.'

'Well,' Eric said again. This time you could hear he was having an argument.

'If you know this Dr Schweitzer whoever he is, and someone came and asked to meet him, I'd bet you'd run inside and hide for about three hours,' Sally said to her brother.

Now Strydom himself arrived, walking in that funny way with his big brown legs thrown outwards, his shorts the colour of cement, his bare feet thick with dust and his blond hair swept back, full and gleaming. My mother always said he was a decent-looking man. 'If you don't look at the lips, Martin.' And my father said, 'I hardly think he's of an age to look at people's mouths, Monica.' Which was just about par for the course in a conversation between my mother and father. Mr Strydom was wide, blond and smiling. His lips were like any other person's lips, really. But they were broad like everything else about him, and hard. That was Strydom all over; as if behind the skin there was more bone than you might expect.

'What the hell, Winnie! What are you doing here? The boy's supposed to be building my rockery, not playing games in the back yard.'

'The dog's got their ball,' said Mrs Strydom.

'Genghis! Drop it!' The order was rammed home with a cuff of the beast's left ear. Genghis dropped the ball. Precious sprang forward, picked it up and rubbed it in the sand to clean it and then on his shorts.

'Precious, give the little master the ball,' said Strydom.

Precious tossed it to Eric.

'Now, you black square on the hypotenuse,' said Strydom with a big wide grin, 'get into the garden before I use your head for a football. And you kids, shove off!' He swung his leg after the departing leper who took the force of his foot smack in the tail and lifted with the shock into a gallop, passing us at speed and heading for the rockery.

'He's got a screw loose,' said Mrs Strydom.

'He's a bloody good worker, when he's not interfered with,' her husband replied.

'He's diseased,' said his wife. 'In head and body.'

Tony gave us a happy look, and we shoved off.

Mrs Strydom was out on that dusty patch by the naked fence soon after breakfast each day. She didn't do anything herself but she ordered Precious around. Strydom worked in the City Engineer's Department and he left off at about seven every morning in his off-white sportscoat with the flecks like burnt toast and his tin sandwich box under his arm. She waved from the garden but he never looked back after he walked down the road with that punchy step, like a kick boxer.

From sun-up Precious was out in the rockery. We saw him as we left for school and he'd grin and leap about in the horse fashion because that's what he remembered of our last meeting. The sun was warm on his pink patches, and his little nose and the bit of ear looked more sad than scary. When we got back home after lunch Mrs Strydom was usually bossing him around again. The soil was as hard as iron and full of shale. Precious had to dig a trench and sieve the stony ground to make the earth foundation of the rockery. Next, the rocks were set in place. Then Mrs Strydom would plant out succulents and cacti in the topsoil sold by Errol.

Sammie came by reading a book.

'Ma says you're not to read and walk at the same time,' said Eric.

Sammie sat down on the ground and went on reading.

'Did you know that old Strydom has a leper working for him?' Tony asked Errol. 'That's him, making the rockery.'

The topsoil man paused, his shovel deep in the dark, damp mossy load, smelling of leaves and alive with pink, fat earthworms. 'But why hire a leper? I wouldn't.'

'Because they're cheap,' said Tony.

'What good is cheap if it dies?' Errol went on spading topsoil.

It was Errol who let us take a peep into the room in the back yard. He did it by offering himself up to Genghis, putting one foot on Strydom's fence and the other on the back of his truck and standing there spooning topsoil into the yard. The sight of a man up on the fence drove Genghis crazy and while he howled and slavered we moved round and took a quick look. The leper's room was almost bare. Coloured pictures were tacked to the wall. Durban beach. And General Jan Smuts, wearing full uniform. There was a sliver of freckled mirror. The bed was made of iron, had no mattress and only a few grey blankets. A chipped enamel basin waited under the window. It wasn't much of a place but then as Eric said, 'What do you expect if you're a leper?'

Eric told his mother about Strydom's leper. It was a bad move. She told all the other mothers and the mothers talked. Then they walked in circles around the front fence of the Strydoms' house where Precious, never seeing them inspecting him, his head down, dug and sieved and shifted rocks.

Their advice to us was pretty various. My mother said: 'I don't want you anywhere near that boy, do you hear me, Martin?' My father said: 'What does it matter if he goes close to him, Monica? Leprosy is not like 'flu, you know.' And Eric's ma simply refused to believe it. 'You don't get lepers here. They'd never allow it. Damn it, we have enough trouble as it is with rag-and-bone men and dustmen and burglars in the bluegums. Lepers! That would be the last straw!'

Tony and Sally's mother was always on the move. She drove her powder-blue Austin A40 and wore an anxious frown which creased her pretty forehead. For years I thought she must be a nurse, always on the way to the site of some accident. But it turned out later that she sold perfumes and lipsticks. She took them along to Swirsky and asked him if he had something to dust her kids with? Swirsky said she wasn't to worry. She wasn't worried. If the good Lord intended her family to get leprosy, then there was no fighting it. But she wanted to be careful. And she was on the road a lot herself.

'You only get lepers further north,' Swirsky promised.

'I dare say he knows what he's talking about,' my mother told my father. 'He travels endlessly. I dare say he's been north.'

Tony and Sally's mother said you couldn't be too careful. And my mother said, right, who was to say that one of the lepers from further north had not slipped into the country. We might wake up one morning to find some of the children had caught it. Too late to cry then.

'I took Martin to Swirsky after he touched that pink creature Errol found. You remember the creature? And, honestly, Swirsky couldn't have cared less. Of course if something happens to their own, then there is no expense spared.'

They decided to dust Sally and Tony with athlete's foot powder 'just in case'.

Sally liked to get really close to Precious. She'd slip in while he worked and sit down next to him. At first she did it for a dare, and then just as a matter of course, as a way of driving her brother crazy.

'Do you realize that you could catch what he's got, and rot?'

Sally's response was to pat Precious on the shoulder which had the effect of making him go into his horse mode. We stood by the fence and watched. Eric sometimes tossed him his tennis ball and Precious threw it back. Tony covered his face when this happened. We had to watch out for Mrs Strydom, so we confined visiting hours to the afternoon when she went inside for lunch and a lie-down. We had to be especially careful when Strydom came home, in the early evening, swinging his lunch tin and calling out to Precious, 'Well, how's it going, my boy? My old son of a compass? My old black set square?'

You could tell that he was an engineer.

Strydom obviously wasn't worried about infection. He

touched Precious often. He liked to cuff him about with his open hand and Precious would throw up his hands to his bit of nose and piece of ear and shout back: 'No, no, my master! My master that isn't nice!' And if Precious had done something wrong then Strydom would grab him by the hair and twist his head down to about knee level and lead him around the rockery pointing out his mistakes, the wrong plants, the wrong rocks.

But he didn't mean anything by it. We had this from Precious himself. He galloped over to us when Mrs Strydom went indoors for lunch. 'Hello, my babies. Have you come to visit Precious? Yoh! But it is too hot!' He spoke quite well, for a leper.

Only Sammie turned up his nose. He was reading about American paratroopers in Italy: *Those Devils in Baggy Pants*. Eric said Sammie had stuck a kitchen knife in his sock and pretended it was a bayonet. His ma beat them both when she found out.

'You wouldn't like it if you were a leper,' Sally said.

'He's a big act, that's all.' Sammie walked off, reading his book.

Sally hated it when Strydom hit him. 'I hope he didn't hurt you, Precious.'

The leper gave his horsey laugh. 'No, no, missy. Boss Strydom is a good boss. He loves Precious. When we have built this rockery, he is going to send Precious on holiday to the sea.'

Sally's sharp intake of breath was painful to hear. 'That's the meanest thing I ever heard, Mart. Can you believe it? Strydom sending the leper on holiday? I think it's cruel to make him think that.'

We stood in the school playground while the headmaster shouted at us over the loudspeaker mounted on the roof. He told us to look up to our parents. Eric whispered to Tony that that was like looking up to Hitler. Tony began laughing. A teacher pulled him out of the line and boxed his ears and Tony began crying. Then the headmaster put on a recording of 'The Whistler and His Dog' and we all marched into our classrooms.

It went on, for about a week, with Precious out in the garden building the rockery and us hanging over the fence. 'Hello, my babies,' Precious called out to us when we passed on our way to school.

When we got back from school Mrs Strydom would be out in the garden screaming, 'The ivy goes in here, not there! And the aloes must be planted, Precious, not buried!'

She caught sight of Sammie and said, 'What are you staring at, Mr Four-Eyes?'

Sammie held up *Those Devils in Baggy Pants.* 'I'm reading, Mrs Strydom.'

Tony said to his sister: 'Maybe you're right about the seaside. They'd never allow a leper on the beach. Soon as he took off his clothes everyone would know. There's probably more of him missing under his clothes.'

Mrs Strydom said to Sammie, 'You'll ruin your eyes. You're far too young to be wearing glasses.'

'You're stupid,' Sally whispered to Tony. 'Precious is never going to the sea. Not because he's a leper but because Mr Strydom's a liar.'

One morning the rockery was finished. All the flowers were planted, the pinks and phlox, cacti and the dwarf pomegranate and the juniper tree. Precious was hopping about like mad, very excited. At about four o'clock, while Mrs Strydom was indoors, he began to get ready for Strydom's homecoming. He began watering the garden. Perhaps this was his own idea. Perhaps he believed that when you have made a garden you water it. It made a kind of sense, I suppose, to a leper.

The topsoil Errol had supplied turned suddenly to mud;

there were small washaways and rockslides. When a stone went it knocked over others. Precious ran from rock to rock trying to push them straight. He was so frantic that he didn't see or hear Mrs Strydom coming.

We had been playing cricket at Tony's place. Sally had just bowled her brother when Eric came along. Eric had stopped trying to learn to juggle and was concentrating what he called his 'forces' on magicians' tricks. He had made this funnel, rolled from newspaper, and carried a plastic jug full of milk. The idea was that you poured the milk into the funnel, unwrapped the paper and, hey presto! the milk was gone.

'You pour, Tone.' Eric gave him the jug.

Tony refused. 'I'm not going to be the one who cops it when they discover you've stolen the milk.'

Sally said, 'You banana,' and poured the milk herself.

Eric stood there holding the funnel at the end of a stiff arm, like an Olympic runner carrying the flaming torch, except that this wasn't a torch, it was a column of milk wrapped in a week old copy of the *Johannesburg Star*. Sally laughed. 'The milk's coming through the paper!'

And it was. The type got very black, you could almost read it. 'It'll work in a moment,' Eric said, 'give it time.'

Behind us we heard Mrs Strydom screaming blue murder but you don't pay too much attention when you're waiting to see if a guy can make a gallon of milk disappear.

Eric's funnel was almost transparent. You could see the level of the milk on the other side of the paper. I could read a headline now: WHO MURDERED BUBBLES SCHROEDER? Suddenly his funnel collapsed in his fist, like a top-heavy flower and milk streamed all over his bare feet. He stared at the mess with tears in his eyes and his mouth set hard. 'Damn it! Damn it,' he said again. 'I'll get it right one day. Just you wait.'

That's when we wandered over to Strydom's fence and saw Precious lying on the ground. The rockery had fallen and big stones lay near. Precious did not move a muscle.

Mrs Strydom saw us. 'The rocks fell on him. What did he expect if he watered it like that?'

We didn't answer her. Precious didn't move. After a while she shrugged and went inside to phone her husband.

We were watching from our fence when Strydom came home. He was whistling 'Sugarbush' but stopped the moment he saw Precious. He inspected the collapsed rockery and walked around the leper once or twice. Then he went over to the tap and switched on the hose. He sprayed Precious from head to foot, very hard, like he was trying to clean him or something. Precious began to move. He kept trying to roll out of the way of the hosepipe. But Strydom kept the water on him. At last Precious staggered to his feet and tried to push a few more rocks into place.

'Go to your room, you old black theodolite,' said Strydom, 'you've done enough damage for one day.'

The next day passed without sign of Precious. Strydom came home and repaired his rockery. He saw us hanging over the fence. 'Hello kiddies.' We just stared back, there was nothing to say. Precious didn't show up the following day either. Or the day after that. A week passed and we had no sign of him. Sally got it into her head that she would check out his little room in the back yard, but first there was the problem of Genghis. Eric volunteered to feed the dog his tennis balls. Sally kissed him. 'It's OK,' said Eric. 'It's probably the last time you'll see me.'

We went over the fence just after nightfall. Tony refused to come but he lent us his torch. 'If you get caught, I'll say it isn't mine.' The torchlight showed a bare room. Everything had gone,

71

the photos of Durban beach, Jan Smuts, the mirror, even the bed had vanished. The room was swept bare.

We sat around on Tony's lawn one hot Tuesday afternoon and looked up at the hawks circling.

'Sally thinks Precious is dead.'

'But we saw him on his feet,' Eric objected. 'We saw him walk into his room.'

'He's gone,' said Sally. 'He was so badly hurt when the rocks fell on him. His room's empty.'

'If he's dead, where did they put him, tell me that?' Tony wanted to know, full of facts and questions as always. 'I mean, if people die they don't just lie around, you know.'

'He's gone to the seaside,' Sammie said. 'What's the bet?'

'Mr Strydom's been extending his rockery,' Sally said.

This sent Tony crazy. He laughed, low and hard, and went on doing it for minutes after the rest of us had told him to shut up. In fact he got so carried away and so determined to prove that this was rubbish that he said he would go and ask Strydom himself. Straight out. Just like that. Man to man.

'Right,' we said, all together.

'Well—' Tony shifted a bit and rubbed his stomach. But we had him and he knew it. The very next morning as Strydom was working in the rockery Tony walked slowly over to the fence. 'Please, Mr Strydom – what happened to Precious?'

Strydom slowly straightened and grinned. 'Why he's gone on holiday, boy, to the coast. Precious is at this moment paddling his tootsies in the Indian Ocean. The lucky son of a compass! I wish it was me. Don't you wish it was you?'

Tony said he did.

'Well Tone?' his sister asked when he came back to us and told us. 'What do you think?'

Tony's eyes clouded over. 'I think, Sal,' he said carefully, like he was giving the question careful consideration, 'I think Precious is dead and buried in the rockery.'

Well, we had to tell someone. Eric spoke to his ma. She fetched him one in the eye. 'You want to talk to me of dead lepers? In the neighbour's garden?' Eric cried when he told us this: 'I'll disappear one day, I swear I will. For ever!'

Sammie also copped it from his ma. 'This is something you've got from those damn books of yours. Read, read, read! It's all you ever do. One day I'll dump the whole load of books in the dustbin. I promise I will.'

My father simply laughed. 'The boy's gone missing, that's all. Boys do. Maybe he's gone to join the burglars living in the bluegums. Maybe Strydom fired him. Life's too short to worry about missing servants. You'll find that out when you get to my age.'

And Sally's mother wouldn't even listen, she just drove off in her Austin and didn't look back.

I suppose about a week must have passed and we were still no closer to knowing what to do. We were sitting out on Tony's front lawn one afternoon nibbling blades of grass when a shadow fell on us and a voice said: 'Hello, my babies!' Smiling he was, his nose and ears looked scrappier than ever, his pink patches were bigger, but he was well and beaming. Precious carried two Rose's lime juice bottles filled with cloudy water. The bottles were stopped with screws of newspaper. We just lay there and stared up at him, against the blue sky his face was a black mask. He'd been down to the coast for the promised holiday. In case there was any doubt about that, he carried the proof. Precious rubbed his stomach and pretended to drink from one of the bottles.

'Water from the sea! You drink and your stomach feels much better!' He gave the bottles to Sally and galloped across the road.

And it was. There was even a shell and a scattering of sand in each bottle.

After that Precious and Strydom were out in the garden almost every day, adding flowers to the rockery. Sally had been right. Strydom had extended it by at least another six feet. Precious was happy and looking very well. He didn't wear the shorts and tunic any longer either. He wore old grey flannels and a white shirt and a straw hat. He stopped galloping on the spot. Strydom didn't stop hitting him or calling him things like 'black son of the set square'. But you could tell something had changed, they got on in a curious way.

And we went back to playing cricket. Tony was the only one to try drinking the sea water and he spent hours in the lavatory. When he came out he'd been reading a little book called *Tanks – Book One*.

A few days later Eric ran away from home and was found sitting crying in the afternoon matinée of *The Creature from the Black Lagoon* in a cinema on the far side of town.

Sammie finished *Those Devils in Baggy Pants*, made himself a parachute from his bedsheet and practised jumping off the branch of a bluegum tree.

It must have been a week, at least, maybe more, before anyone noticed that Mrs Strydom was missing.

Tony went crazy. Just like he'd gone crazy about Precious the leper. And nothing any of us could say would persuade him to leave it alone. He went over the fence late one night, into the Strydoms' yard, carrying his torch, and in considerable risk of being chewed by Genghis, the flesh-eating horse. He was back about twenty minutes later.

'She lives in the room. Where Precious lived. She's got a bed and a chair and a cupboard with a mirror.'

'Like a prisoner?' I asked. I could hear how silly I sounded but I couldn't help myself. I heard myself say again: 'Like a prisoner?'

'She gets up and cooks their breakfast. She's up before dawn. She works in the house till late at night and then she goes back to her room. That's why we haven't seen her.'

'You mean – like a servant?' Sally's eyes were wide and blue. 'And Precious has moved into the house?'

Everywhere in the universe servants lived in the room in the back yard. No one in the entire galaxy had a Mrs Strydom in the back yard. But you couldn't argue with the laughter. We could hear it in the early evenings, long and loud, it floated out of the Strydoms' house, across the rockery, across the fence and into Eric's living-room where we sat playing pick-up sticks. Eric's ma was coming up from behind, going for the black. You heard it clear as a bell, men laughing.

ARRIVEDERCI!

NICODEMUS was a big giver.

And this was odd, he being so skinny. His tunic was cut across his chest and there seemed next to nothing to the man. Just these little arms, legs and bare feet in the long baggy shorts.

He came with the house. If he hadn't coughed when we went into the garage, 'I'd never have found him!' my father told Gus Trupshaw. When we moved to Badminton, he was stored in the darkness along with broken ladders and a case of Trotter's jellies 'from the heart of South Africa'. The lime-green powders in their yellow boxes had grown as hard as cakes of soap because the damp had got to them. There was also an advertisement for New Consolidated Goldfields which included amongst its directors Sir G.S. Harvie-Watt, Bt., TD, QC, MP. I used to say the name to myself in all its crackling glory late at night when I was in bed and sleep wouldn't come and I thought of vampires and death and burglars in the bluegum trees, where the estate sloped into a little frothing river. Beyond the river and the bluegums the red, hard-iron ground stretched away to a range of hot, rough hills.

The burglars in the bluegums haunted the estate. Men slept with their service revolvers beside their beds. When butter and flour disappeared from pantries or booze vanished from liquor cabinets, people said their servants were related to the burglars and they whispered that the burglars were good at taking impressions of keys in cakes of soap. The dogs got bigger. Attila and Julius and Adolf slavered in the back yards. And when they found no burglars to bite, they bit the neighbours instead, or visiting aunts, or each other. Fathers leapt from their beds in the small hours and ran naked into the velvet African night blasting away with their pistols. I never saw a burglar. But I believed in them, the way I believed in God and Sir G.S. Harvie-Watt, Bt., TD, QC, MP.

Then Margot van Reen became a widow. She lived a few doors away with her husband Alec who had come back from the War a full lieutenant and begun building a rockery along the front fence. He keeled over one day just as he was planting out some Namaqualand daisies for winter flowering.

My father blamed the government. 'That's what we get. The soldier's reward. This is a damn silly country. I went off to fight the Nazis and I came back to find that the place was being run by dyed-in-the-wool fascists. Thanks for nothing!'

When Mrs van Reen lost her husband she walked about in the rain without appearing to notice. She wore white a lot and with her blonde hair and pale face this made her look as if she was made of mist. She never cleaned her windows. And if you met her in the street and said, 'Good morning, Mrs van Reen,' she would turn away and cry. And if you said, 'How are you?' – she'd say things like, 'I long for winter. Autumn was nearly the finish of me.' And then, if you really tried, and you said to her, 'We're in November already,' she would turn her face up to the sky, flutter her eyes, and her lips would move as if she was praying to someone.

'Feel free, Margot. Take him whenever the spirit moves.' My father had marched Nicodemus over to Mrs van Reen's house and pushed him at her. 'He isn't trained for anything. But take him. With my compliments. He can do a bit around the house. Or in the garden. He's not the brightest but he's keen and he doesn't need anything.'

That was true. In his small room behind our garage he slept on a thin blue mattress on an iron bedstead. He had two uniforms of white calico, big loose shorts, tunics cut square at the neck, and shorts edged in red piping. A mirror framed in red plastic hung from a nail and beside it he had pasted a photograph, cut from a newspaper of Mussolini in military uniform.

'This is a happy fat chap!' Nicodemus pointed at the dictator. Then he brought his own face close to his mirror. 'And this is a silly thin chap.'

Nicodemus could only give. He had a force inside him that made him tend that way. It was like he had a list to starboard or a bad leg. He made and gave. Catapults were his speciality, the Y-piece cut from the green branch of the bluegum, stripped of its bark and then sun-dried. The rubber he took from old inner tubes and for a sling he used the tongues from his own sand shoes.

'My godfathers!' my mother cried when she saw him hobbling about in his tongue-less shoes. 'That's the last time I provide him with decent footwear!'

He loved French knitting. I wore a tall gum-pink hat around the estate for days until my mother told me to take it off because Gus Trupshaw said I was growing up like a 'pansy'. And then a few days later I ran into Eric in the dark little wood behind Swirsky's pharmacy and he cut open the back of my hand with a piece of glass, saying as he did so, 'That's what you get for wearing a pink hat.' I walked home to Nicodemus, not hurting much, but puzzled and rather worried about the blood splashing on my legs. He stopped the bleeding and bandaged it so beautifully I really did cry.

When my mother saw me she screamed and marched me straight up to Swirsky for a professional opinion. She was doing this more often now that Swirsky had 'settled down'. He'd passed his first year. It was 1951, the beginning of a brand-new decade. Maybe Swirsky had decided he had something to contribute. Maybe he'd stay, and not 'do a flit'.

'I really don't know what this child has done to himself. Honestly, Martin! All this *and* Christmas almost on us. What will you think of next?'

My mother dreaded Christmas. She spent much of the year worrying about it. I always felt it was something that blew up on the horizon, like a thunderstorm.

Swirsky, in his white coat, ironed wafer-thin, took off the wrappings and examined the wound. 'It's clean. And the dressing is a beautiful job.'

'It ought to be,' my mother replied grimly, 'that was my best tea-towel. Irish linen, if you please. Thank you very much, Mr Nicodemus!'

Whenever Nicodemus had done something beautiful he liked to go down on his knees, lean back and crouch on his haunches, blow out his cheeks and pop his eyes. I knew what he meant. The silly thin chap had become the happy fat chap – he had turned into Mussolini. He certainly got on with things at Margot van Reen's place. He cleaned the windows and finished building the rockery while she watched from the kitchen window as if, perhaps, she expected the curse that killed her husband to fell Nicodemus too.

We invited her over for Christmas lunch and I remember how she smiled at my father across the turkey. 'Your Nicodemus! He's a champ!'

'I hope he's not giving you any trouble,' said my mother. 'Martin, sit up straight and try not to breathe when you eat.

Nicodemus cooked our lunch. Mind you, I have to watch him every inch of the way.'

Nicodemus arrived with a plate of steaming pumpkin. Mrs van Reen waved, a little windmill wave, as if she was polishing a mirror. Nicodemus showed his teeth through the steam, then he bowed with one hand behind his back and laid the plate in front of Margot van Reen like a butler or a real waiter.

When he'd left my father said, 'He's not a bad old stick.'

'He's a dear,' said Margot van Reen. 'He's my good fairy.'

Later that afternoon we all went to the Christmas party in the kindergarten. Swirsky was Father Christmas. At first there'd been some on the estate who'd objected to that because he was Jewish. But Swirsky said, 'Don't think of me as Jewish – I'm neutral.'

He looked fat and angry in his red robe and hood and woolly whiskers. 'I'll take Sally first!' His grey trousers hung beneath the robe.

When Nicodemus turned up and sat at the back on the floor, Swirsky pulled off his hood and I saw how his own moustache refused to lie down under the cottonwool moustache. It looked angry and sharp, like an assassin's knife.

'*Sayonara!*' He pointed at the door. '*Arrivederci!*'

'Can I read my letter to Father Christmas?' Sally wanted to know.

Everyone turned round. You could tell from his language that Mr Swirsky really liked to travel. His moustache looked sharper than ever. It seemed to be planning a war.

'He's not doing any harm.' The voice spoke from the back of the room where all the grown-ups were standing. 'It's Christmas, Mr Swirsky.'

Swirsky stood up and clapped his hand to his woollen eyebrows and stared at Margot van Reen as if she were a pirate ship

83

on the distant horizon. 'OK, OK. But let's get this straight, folks, I'm not having him on my lap.'

All the grown-ups laughed. And so did Nicodemus.

Without waiting to be told Sally went ahead and read her letter.

Dear Father Christmas,
Could you give me a tent and a sponge and a chair
and a skipping rope and that is all –
Love from Sally

Swirsky pulled on his hood and hit his beard to make it stick. Then he pulled Sally on to his knee. 'Waddya think this is – Christmas?'

He gave her a beach ball. All the grown-ups laughed again. Nicodemus lifted his head like he'd seen a vision and tears poured down his cheeks.

'Oh happy days!' said my father. 'Who the hell asked sad sack to the party?'

'I did,' said Margot van Reen.

It was some time in January when I met Mrs van Reen in Henry Street. She was dressed in blue silk and winked at me. 'Nicodemus is building me a bower of bliss. I feel like the Lady of Shalott. I've felt that way ever since Alec died. I've been pining for the return of my knight.'

By February it was there, a summerhouse, and Nicodemus had sunk the posts and set up a trellis and planted sweet-peas and a creeper called peachadilla which Mrs van Reen said would flower in July. She sat in her summerhouse and drank tea out of small blue cups.

One evening I found Nicodemus lying on his bed wearing a full white beard which hooked on behind his ears. He was staring into the mirror and smiling. When he saw me he patted my hand. 'Happy! Happy, my little lord.' Then he rolled over again and stared into the mirror. His beard was fat and flowing. His eyes were wide. He looked at the picture of Mussolini and he looked at himself and I could see how happy he was.

Then the presents started appearing on the doorsteps in the mornings. There were French-knitted scarves; there were catapults and kites; there were reed flutes and little bicycles constructed from coathangers and they all came wrapped in Christmas paper. It was the paper Nicodemus had collected from the floor on the day that Swirsky gave out the presents.

'Someone has it in for us,' said Gus Trupshaw. 'For God's sake how can you be having Christmas in February?'

My father snorted, 'Can you imagine where we'll be by July?'

'Please *do* something, Gordon,' my mother said.

'What do you suggest, Monica?' my father asked. 'Shall I call in the Army?'

And Gus Trupshaw said, 'Spot on, Gordon!'

The Torch Commando began nightly patrols. They fetched their dogs. Their torches burnt into the darkness and they were happy again. Suddenly they were out at night with a chance of catching all the burglars in the bluegums. It was a bit like the War – they were chasing Germans again. All the dogs which had bitten the neighbours and the aunts and each other now had something real to hunt. There were shots fired, though Gus Trupshaw said afterwards they'd been blanks.

They ran him to earth in Mrs van Reen's garden. To escape the dogs he climbed on to the roof of the summerhouse and crawled to the edge and peered into the darkness. He kept his hand pressed to his forehead trying to see beyond the bright torches.

Margot van Reen ran out of her front door wearing a pink

nightdress. She kicked my father, she bit Gus Trupshaw. But the hunters ignored her. They began shaking the trellis, they trampled the peachadilla creeper; they snapped the sweet-peas. And once they had him in hand they drove him away in a Morris Minor with a blanket over his head.

'To save him from the dogs,' said Gus Trupshaw.

'You bastards,' screamed Margot van Reen. 'What have you done with his beard?'

Afterwards she seemed fine. She never mentioned Nicodemus. She started smiling. By May she was saying happily, 'Autumn! A lovely season, don't you think? So fruitful!' She wore red dresses and straw hats.

One day in June Swirsky came to see my mother and his moustache was at its most dangerous. It was pressed to his nose like a pirate's throwing knife. He and my mother went into the kitchen and locked the door. As he was leaving the house I heard him say: 'I'm *en route.*'

My mother said quietly, 'Will she have it?'

'Too far gone to stop it. She came to the pharmacy wanting something for her swollen legs. Oh yes, she's having it and she's pleased as punch. And she's staying.'

'And you're heading out?' my mother asked.

'Cape Town,' Swirsky said. 'It's just that I thought you should be told.'

'Why me?'

'Well, he was yours. It seemed right you should be the first to know.'

'I didn't ask for him,' said my mother very frostily. 'I told you before – he came with the house.'

She told my father, 'It's all very well for him. Swirsky can

86

come and go as he pleases. He's a bachelor. But what about the rest of us?'

'Jesus wept!' said my father.

Every night I said my prayers to make it stop. I asked God. I asked Sir G.S. Harvie-Watt, Bt., TD, QC, MP of New Consolidated Goldfields. Meanwhile she got bigger and bigger. Nicodemus had left us something. We watched it. We looked away. But it wouldn't stop.

It was something coming to us.

PATTERNS

WHEN Swirsky loaded up his '51 Ford, turned his key into the new key-turn starting, and drove away in the direction of the dynamite factory, we never expected to see him again.

'Why Cape Town?' my father had wanted to know, when Swirsky shut up his shop and told everyone he was leaving Badminton. My father said it as if Cape Town was his worst enemy. 'What's bloody Cape Town got?'

'Gateway to Africa,' said Swirsky.

'Never in a hundred years,' my father said.

'Give it ten,' said Swirsky. 'By 1961 Cape Town will be another New York. I'll put money on it.'

Because he couldn't find a buyer for his pharmacy he turned to Papas from the Greek Tea Room. And Papas turned to his family connections. From a brother-in-law, who ran a used-car lot in Orange Grove, he got hold of two big wooden crates. They broke up the wooden crates in Swirsky's back yard, working with crowbars beneath the loquat tree. Then they boarded up Swirsky's pharmacy. The planks covering the windows were stamped in the sort of blue ink you saw on sides of beef: *Duly & Co. Ford Cars, Trucks and Tractors. For all Your Motoring Requirements In the Two Rhodesias.*

'Two Rhodesias!' Swirsky said to Papas as they sat beneath

the loquat tree, crowbars resting like rifles on their shoulders. 'If one doesn't make it, there will always be a spare.'

Sally and I stood outside the blind windows of Swirsky's pharmacy feeling pretty strange after he left. Under the loquat tree the yellow fruit lay in the grass among splinters and sawdust. Reminders that Swirsky had been here – and that now he was gone. Signs that hurt the heart.

The back of his car had been loaded with tins of babyfood and boxes of Dr McKenzie's Venoids. I pictured him somewhere on the road to Cape Town, his face faintly green in the light from the 'Safety-Glow' control panel. I felt lonely. There would be no more trees built from bottles of laxatives. Forests of California Syrup of Figs climbing in his windows. No more mediaeval castles constructed from Carter's Little Liver Pills.

It went on hurting each time we saw the splinters and the sawdust beneath the loquat tree where Swirsky and Papas had rested the day they boarded up the place. Only when the rains came and washed away the signs of where he had been did we somehow feel a little better about his going. But for some reason feeling better about his going also made us feel worse.

Sally said she would write to him and ask him to come back to Badminton. Tony said we didn't have an address for him and that she was wasting her time. Sally wrote anyway. She sent a letter addressed to Mr Nathan Swirsky, Cape Town. She wrote three times and never had a reply. Then she wrote to the Leopard Rock Motel in Rhodesia, and from there she had a reply telling her that Swirsky had travelled to England.

'I might have known,' said my mother, 'Cape Town wasn't good enough for him.'

It was about this time that the new Jewish Old Age Home started receiving its first guests.

'Typical,' said my mother, 'Nathan Swirsky was very careful not to be here when his friends started moving in.'

I was puzzled by this. If the people moving into the Home were his friends why wouldn't he want to be there to see them? My mother said it was because some friends were more trouble than they were worth.

We began to see the people from the Jewish Old Age Home using the Greek Tea Room, and the Rug Doctor and the Bottle Store. There was Mrs Raubenheimer, who wore blue glasses and a red hat with a veil. And old Dr Moishe who always wore a suit and a black hat. And blind Mr Levine who walked with a white stick. They all seemed very friendly and so we asked them if they'd heard from Swirsky.

Mrs Raubenheimer made a round, red O with her lips and asked, 'Who is Mr Swirsky?'

And Sally said, 'A friend of yours. He used to run the chemist's shop.'

Dr Moishe said he knew a Swirsky, Morris Swirsky. 'Was he some relation?'

My mother said that these people had only been in Badminton for two minutes and you would have thought that they owned the place.

Dr Moishe took Gus Trupshaw and my father to his golf club and when they came home my father told my mother that old Moishe was a pukka bloke and Gus Trupshaw said he was a real white man.

'Their ways may not be our ways. But any man who can chip out of the rough for a birdie on the seventeenth is a man I take my hat off to every time.'

My father set up a putting area on the lawn and he bought himself plus-fours and a yellow cardigan. He said that Dr Moishe knew Bobbie Locke personally and Bobbie Locke was the sort of man who made you proud to be a South African.

'That's what I mean,' said Gus Trupshaw. 'He has standards.'

My mother said she had nothing against standards. And she had nothing against people as people. But she very much hoped that this wasn't the start of some pattern.

My mother started talking about patterns more often. There were patterns in everything, she said. Not one door closed but another opened. God's ways were mysterious. When the floods came and washed away half my father's garden, she said that there was probably something wrong with the weather. Life was full of things we could not understand. Look at Margot van Reen's dilemma. Had Margot van Reen ever imagined, when her husband died so suddenly, that she would be facing this dilemma? Poor little baby and Heaven knew what its prospects were? But Margot van Reen had done what she did and we would all have to take the consequences.

Sometimes, when she was alone with me, she would begin crying and asked what would happen if my father died like Margot van Reen's husband. I said I would look after her. She said she hoped the pattern of our lives would allow that. I said I would buy her diamonds when I was bigger. But she said it didn't have to be diamonds, pearls would do. But, in the mean time, had I noticed that the Indian vegetable seller who visited Badminton every week was selling very green avocados? What did I make of that? Or that the Hendersons, over in Elizabeth Crescent, had been burgled for the third time in a row? Did I know that the Bible talked about the last days, when the world would be destroyed by fire and flood? It was written there, she said, in the Bible. It was a pattern . . .

One Friday, around three, we lost Eric's little brother Sammie, down at the clay wall in the bluegum plantation. To begin with it had been a good day, down by the river. We were tunnelling into the clay wall and Sammie had got in almost two yards. It looked like being a record. Before we started tunnelling we had been having a clay fight, stripping long whips from the weeping willows that hung down over the stream, fixing clay balls to the end of our whips and then letting fly. You could knock a guy down if you hit him plumb centre. Sammie had been a whizz at clay fights despite wearing glasses. Deadly over about fifteen feet. Even though he was short for his age and a couple of years younger than the rest of us, he was the shortest, most lethal nine-year-old in Badminton.

Perhaps being short, and a bit blind, made him such a good tunneller. He'd taken off his glasses before he began digging, because his ma had said she would kill him if he smashed them. Sammie had got his nose right up against the wall of his tunnel when the bank collapsed. We dug like furies but there was too much clay. By the time we got him out he'd been dead ten minutes. But he looked perfect. Tony started crying and wanted to run away but Sally said she'd kill him, stone dead, if he did. So Tony stayed but he went on crying. Eric said he'd better call his ma. But when he said perhaps we should clean him first I knew he did not want to call his mother. So I said I would do it and Eric said, 'OK, if you want to.'

We washed the clay off him. It was an odd thing to do but we felt responsible. How could we hand him over looking so grey and clayey? We weren't supposed to be down by the clay bank anyway because of the burglars who hid in the bluegums and might steal us. Sammie had looked so smooth and clean after we'd washed him. We put on his glasses. That made it worse in a way because it seemed that he was quietly asleep. Tony, who had stopped crying, told us what we did not want to hear: he wasn't going to wake up. Then I went to fetch Eric's ma. I didn't want to do it and I wished I hadn't offered. Everyone was crying by then except for me. I couldn't cry because Eric's ma would have guessed something terrible had happened even before I told her.

When his ma saw Sammie's body lying on the clay bank she cried out: 'He didn't even break his glasses!' like she was mad and glad all at once.

Eric took Sammie's death in a funny way. He kept on building these houses or shelters, or shacks. He would raid one of the half-built homes on the Estate where builder's rubble lay and start building his own house with borrowed bricks. He would cover the roof with corrugated iron, or bits of planking. And then he would brew tea and invite people to visit.

Pretty soon the walls would fall in and he usually got cut up. After it happened to us a couple of times we stopped calling on him. Who wants to go for tea if the roof falls in?

The thing was, that Eric got cut, but he never got seriously hurt and that really seemed to upset him. I guessed that next to Sammie, he felt a failure. Sammie let loose clay balls at the end of his willow whip and we said, 'Jeez, Sam, that one must have gone at about ninety miles an hour!' But Eric never managed more than a lob with his clay whip. And he wasn't much of a tunneller, either. So when Sammie died, Eric tried to follow him. Roofs fell in on him but he never got more than scratched. Sometimes he talked of becoming a magician. He was planning to make himself disappear. But until that happened, he kept on building these houses.

When Eric's ma found out about the collapsing houses she put a stop to it. For the rest of the year she kept an eye on him. She met the school bus in the afternoons, as if he was a baby again. 'Where I go, he goes,' she said. 'He has caused enough grief to last a lifetime.' Eric walked home beside her, his head down. Sometimes he would trip and fall, cutting his knees on the sharp gravel in Henry Street, and bleed a bit. It wasn't as good as getting the roof to fall on him. But it was the best he could manage.

And it was still part of the pattern.

We missed Swirsky when Christmas came around. It hadn't been the same since he left.

At Christmas time Eric's ma put on a moustache and a red silk gown and handed out presents from a hessian sack down in the kindergarten hall. We missed Swirsky and his real moustache lying like a hidden stiletto under the soft cottonwool fake. Eric stood beside his ma, wearing a white pillow-case and a coathanger halo, sprayed with silver.

'Eric is the elf who delves,' his ma said, huge as a post-box in her red silk gown. Eric cried all the time and his tears wet the presents.

'Shut up and delve!' his mother kept hissing at him.

But Eric was remembering his little brother Sammie and he cried all the harder so that when we got them the presents felt as though they'd been left out in the rain.

1952 was the year for losing people. We had lost King George. We had lost Nicodemus. We had lost Sammie and now we had lost Swirsky. It seemed rather like the desert war in North Africa. We hung about in front of Swirsky's boarded-up pharmacy for weeks. Mr Benjamin the Rug Doctor came out of his shop and said: 'He's not coming back. He's not Lazarus, you know.'

About the same time my mother began taking a close interest in what she called my 'bits'.

'They shouldn't disappear into the tops of your legs like that, Martin.'

She asked Gus Trupshaw to have a look at them because his

sister was a nurse and she felt that this gave him medical connections.

'I would have asked Mr Swirsky to look at them and decide whether we needed a medical opinion. But he's gone off to the Lord knows where. Thank heavens, Mr Trupshaw and your father were in the Army together. So it's keeping it in the family.'

I had to take my shorts down in Gus Trupshaw's bedroom. He had a picture of General Montgomery on the wall. General Montgomery smiled at me from the frame.

'His eyes watch you as you move about the room,' Gus said. 'That's just the way he watched Rommel in the North African campaign.'

He took a look at me and said I would never make a snooker player. 'Martin fails to pocket the necessary,' said Gus Trupshaw. 'You should see a quack, Monica. His future's at stake.'

My mother took me to see Dr Moishe, at the Jewish Old Age Home, because he was the closest. She said, 'Leave the talking to me, Martin. I don't want this to drag on. It could cost a fortune.'

Dr Moishe said: 'I wouldn't worry. They go up and down. One day Martin's testicles will descend all on their own.'

'Well, I wish they would get a move on,' said my mother.

Once we got outside the consulting room she said to me, 'Now what are we going to do until they descend? Honestly, Martin, you are the giddy limit!'

Other than that nothing seemed to change much in Badminton after Swirsky left. Our fathers went on working in gardens wearing bits of old Air Force and Army uniforms, caps and belts and boots. Sometimes they looked not at all like soldiers, but more like deserters. They cursed the shale and mopped their brows as their dahlias withered. Sally's aunt from Kenya was bitten by an Alsatian named Caesar but it wasn't much of a bite. Though everyone agreed it showed what Caesar might do to a burglar, one day.

Once a month the coalmen came with their hoods of hessian and lifted great nobbled sacks of coal on to their shoulders. Once a week the water truck came, and Mr Govender the vegetable seller. Twice a week the dustbin men came, and with the big dogs like Caesar and Attila and Adolf snapping at their heels, they hoisted the trash cans high on their shoulders and ran lightly down our driveways on black rubber sandals cut from old car tyres.

Then some weeks before Christmas Margot van Reen went away. She had grown very big after Nicodemus left us. She walked around the Estate in a white hat and blue sandals. She was so big you felt it seemed you could see her for miles. Then suddenly she wasn't there. I wondered if she was dead. One night I dreamt that the men on the Estate had gathered her up secretly and driven her away with a blanket over her head. Just like Nicodemus.

Next morning my mother told me I had been walking in my sleep. 'You gave me the most terrible fright, Martin. I woke up in the dead of night and found you standing at the foot of my bed, holding your pillow to your chest. I knew you must be up to no good because when I spoke to you, you didn't answer. Then your father noticed your eyes were closed. We put you back to bed. Minutes later you were up again. Up and down like a yo-yo. Just like your bits.'

I couldn't tell her what I was dreaming about. In case it was true. Then, out of the blue, Tony and I met Margot van Reen pushing a pram along William Street. Beneath what looked like yards of white netting a baby slept.

'This is my Anastasia. She'll be charmed to make your acquaintance when she's a bit older,' said Margot van Reen to Tony and me. 'My Anastasia is a gift from God.'

'I wonder what God would say to that?' my mother asked.

After this she would, from time to time, run her hand across her forehead and tell me that the pattern was clear. My father wanted to know what the pattern was and she told him that if the police were to investigate little Anastasia they were very likely to stumble across his involvement in the matter. They would put two and two together. Had he thought about that?

My father put down the copy of *Life* he'd been reading. 'Here's an article you'd be interested in, Monica. "How the Kremlin treats its own." When I look around me I sometimes think the Kremlin's not as black as it's painted. Look, blame me. I was palooka enough to march up North to fight Jerry. Say I'm soft in the head. Risking my life while the bloody government got under the covers with Messrs Hitler and Mussolini. Tell me I'm wrong to go on believing that this garden of mine can be built into something despite the worst soil in the Transvaal. Call me stupid for fighting a plague of eel-worm as well as floods and scheming Indian topsoil sellers. But please don't connect me with Margot van Reen's fandango.'

'You gave her Nicodemus,' my mother pointed out.

'But I didn't give her the bun in the oven, did I?' said my father.

My mother said that wasn't a very nice thing to be putting into my head and my father said she didn't have to worry about that. From what Dr Moishe had said putting buns in people's ovens was not going to be one of my problems.

I asked Sally what she knew about buns and Sally asked her mother. Next thing a deputation of mothers arrived to see my father and asked him if he was aware that all over Badminton children were talking of buns in the oven.

My mother said, 'I didn't know where to put my face, Gordon. They said – "Is your husband planning to hand out copies of the *Kinsey Report* to the children of Badminton?" '

'Who is Kinsey?' I asked.

My mother's lips closed tight as purse-strings. She sniffed, shooting her eyebrows up towards her hairline. 'Now look what you've done.'

The hail fell in Badminton. It hammered so loudly on the corrugated iron roofs we stuck our fingers in our ears. When the storm had passed hail stones lay inches thick in the garden. They choked the gutters and the drains. My father stood at the window watching it flattening everything he'd planted and he shouted: 'Go to hell in a handbasket!' We picked up handfuls of hail, like white corn off the cob, and pretended it was snow. It melted in our hands and ran through our fingers when we tried to make knobbled snowballs. Badminton turned to mud.

Sally's ma told her that Margot van Reen was an unwed mother. We should feel sorry for her because the man concerned had not married her. We knew this was impossible. Women did not marry their servants. They married men. Anyway, Nicodemus wasn't a man. He was someone who had just come with the house when we bought it.

Tony said that she was jolly lucky that Nicodemus hadn't married her. She might have gone to gaol.

Sally said she didn't care. She missed Nicodemus. She missed Swirsky. She missed Sammie. Sally cried a bit while we watched and then she stopped. She pulled two rubber tennequoit rings up over her knees and under her dress. Then she stalked down Edward Avenue throwing her legs out very wide. Tony said her blood would stop flowing and she'd have to have her legs cut off if she did that. Sally said she didn't care about having her legs cut off. But she stepped out of the tennequoit rings anyway.

My father, Gus Trupshaw and Dr Moishe were down at the ex-servicemen's club in the kindergarten hall. Gus Trupshaw was

101

saying that Nat King Cole, to his mind, was the kind of black man that he could take to in a big way.

'Nat King Cole can sleep in my house any night of the week.'

I sat under the plastic palm tree in the corner. I studied the Viceroy Cigarette advertisement on the paper table cloth. A man in a grey tuxedo, with dark hair combed straight back and a ginger moustache, was lighting the cigarettes of two women in long evening gowns.

Immaculate grooming . . . the art of wearing clothes well . . .
talented repartee . . . these things go hand in hand with the
smoking of Viceroy.

Dr Moishe said, 'I've heard whisper of it. Between you, me and the gatepost, I never believed it. Should I believe it?'

Gus Trupshaw jerked his head towards me. 'Beware big ears on the bandstand.'

'I beg yours?' said Dr Moishe, looking around vaguely.

'No names, no pack drill,' said my father.

'His missus reckons Gordon could be slapped in the jug,' said–Gus Trupshaw. 'As employer of our departed friend. Accessory after the fact. Point is – does your missus want you out of the way?' Gus Trupshaw punched my father on the arm and gave his big laugh. 'She just might shop you herself, Gordon!'

Dr Moishe whistled: 'Not even this government would be that cracked. Another round, gents?'

'Duty calls,' my father shook his head.

'He wants to get home in case his wife gives the cop station a bell,' Gus Trupshaw said.

'Just a quickie, then,' said my father. 'I wouldn't put anything past this bunch of monkeys. Pity the poor sod dandling one of our dusky brethren. A cop jumps out from behind a bush waving a pair of handcuffs. Bang! Straight into the cells.'

Gus Trupshaw poured three more brandies and Cokes and when the others tried to pay him he held up his hands and said, 'No, chaps. This is my shout.'

They'd all settled back with their drinks when Dr Moishe said, 'What happens to Nat King Cole? I mean, if he did spend the night at your place, you could very well have the force breathing down your neck.'

I studied the picture of the tall man lighting cigarettes with the two women. I wondered if they were part of a pattern. I was beginning to believe my mother. There did seem to be a pattern about these things. Where in the world were we to find 'immaculate grooming' of the sort I saw in the picture? How did you join a world where you found men in grey tuxedos making talented repartee? And even if you found one in our world would you find the other? According to the advertisement they always went hand in hand. That was their pattern.

Gus Trupshaw called over to me: 'Hello, Martin. How are the bits?'

Dr Moishe looked up and smiled. 'Martin will be all right,' he said. 'One of these days. Won't you, Martin?'

I nodded but I wasn't so sure.

A few days later Tony and I were strolling down Edward Avenue and we met Margot van Reen. She was crying. The hailstorm had stirred the dust of Edward Avenue into swirls of thick, sticky red mud. And Mrs van Reen was trying to force her way through. She was up to her ankles in the stuff. The pram had sunk to its axles. The baby, golden skin and big dark eyes, sat beneath its foamy netting and tried to put all its fingers into its mouth. Mrs van Reen's shoes had disappeared. She had used one of

Anastasia's nappies and tried to clean the mud from her legs. A couple of filthy nappies lay where she had dropped them. Mrs van Reen looked at us and she cried some more.

Tony and I pulled off our socks and shoes and waded into the bog. We pushed and pulled at the pram until it was free. Margot van Reen stepped out of her shoes which were stuck fast in the ooze. She reached up under her blue dress and we saw her legs were long and white. She took off her stockings.

'It's too ridiculous,' she kept saying. 'I knew I should go back. But I was already late for tea at the Jewish Old Age Home. Mrs Raubenheimer was expecting me. The harder I pushed the more stuck I got. Ghastly goo! Have you ever known the feeling of the pit beneath your feet? I got quite panicky. Thank you, dear men. My knights in shining armour.'

When she'd gone we looked at the nappies lying where she'd flung them. The red sludge was setting firm on the tips of the towelling fibres and made them stand out in whorls of muddy goose-flesh. Only the heels of her shoes were to be seen, so deeply had she trodden them into the mud. It was already glueing itself hard between the tiny squares of her nylon stockings.

We knew we could not leave them where they were. They gave us the feeling that someone had undressed in the middle of Edward Avenue. That's the way it looked. And we'd been there to see it. So we collected everything, and down at the clay bank, beside the river where we'd lost Sammie in the tunnel, we buried Margot van Reen's ruined shoes, Anastasia's nappies and the pair of caked nylons.

And I began to see then that no matter how much you cared for things, they didn't care for you. They had their own ways. And their ways weren't yours. They got you involved and you couldn't help it. They were the pattern you were part of.

★

Margot van Reen met my father some days later and sent greetings to her two 'knights'. My father wanted to know what this meant. My mother said it meant trouble. Look at what had happened the last time Margot van Reen had a knight.

'Martin's safe enough,' my father said. 'He hasn't got his bits yet.'

Soon after that my mother tried to get Swirsky's pharmacy closed down. She said she could not stand the old planks in the window. It was a real eyesore, she said. She got my father to make enquiries but it turned out that Swirsky still owned his shop. So if he wanted to board it up with planks advertising Ford Cars and Tractors in Rhodesia, then that was his privilege.

My mother got that look in her eyes that meant she had something very important to share with us. She took my father and me into the kitchen and carefully closed the door. Then she leaned on the window-sill and stared into the garden. She had had a terrible fright, she told us. She'd been up to the Municipality and studied the architectural designs for the Jewish Old Age Home. She had discovered that it was part of a secret plan.

'You're not aware of it when you first look at it. If you just drive up to it. But see it from above, and the secret becomes clear. From the air. What do you make of that, Gordon?'

My mother's eyes were shining. Her lower lip trembled.

'What do I make of that? I don't make anything of that, Monica,' said my father. 'Sorry to be so dim. What do you make of that, Monica?'

You could see my mother was disappointed. She said she had no idea what to make of it. It was jolly odd. Who was the secret message aimed at? All she knew was that if you flew over Badminton and looked down you wouldn't be able to miss it. It was visible for miles.

'Sorry,' said my father, 'but you've lost me.'

'A giant Star of David. It's right up there, above our heads. I get cold all over just thinking about it. It's a sort of pattern.'

'Pattern?' My father shook his head. 'Talk sense, woman.'

My mother looked at me, 'Martin knows. Don't you, Martin?'

I put my hands in my pockets. There seemed to be patterns everywhere. You couldn't escape them. I thought of the mud hardening in the tiny squares of Margot van Reen's nylon stockings. How the tips of the towelling weave in Anastasia's nappies turned into something else, like a field of iron filings.

My father looked at me. With my hands in my pockets I felt my bits, which might go up and might come down. But I said nothing. I was in enough trouble as it was.

BRAVO!

ERIC saw him first. He'd been sitting on the pavement outside the Rug Doctor's when a big car pulled up. Eric stuffed his book down his shirt and ran to tell us. Sally put the tennis ball in her pocket and Tony dropped his cricket bat. We ran all the way to the pharmacy, but when we got there we felt strange, so we hung back across the road and waited to see if he knew us. I reckon Swirsky must have been away for a couple of years. But it felt like for ever.

Sally did not wait. She dashed across the road and kissed him. Swirsky had always filled his clothes tightly. Now he was wearing yellow shoes, blue trousers and a yellow leather coat that matched his shoes. His clothes seemed fuller than ever. Sally hugged him and cried on his dark green tie.

'Whoa, girlie!' Swirsky lifted her into the air. 'Any more water and you'll melt my moustache.' He put her down carefully and mopped his moustache with his handkerchief. Then he waved his handkerchief at the dark green car parked outside his pharmacy. 'That's the new 1954 Opel Olympia. Straight out of the box. South Africa's most modern car. And that, in the front seat, is the new Mrs Nathan J. Swirsky.'

Tony, Eric and I went on hanging back. Eric had pulled his book out of his shirt and was pretending to read. Tony and I pretended to be watching his reading. His book was called *My Eight Years With The Congo Pygmies*.

109

'Morning men,' Swirsky called. 'Let me tell you something for nothing. When you next meet a Frenchman, say to him, "Bonjour, mon ami" – and you'll have a friend for life.'

Papas from the Greek Tea Room wandered outside to see what all the noise was about.

'Get away with you!' Papas shouted when he saw who it was, grinning all over his face, and hugging Swirsky.

'Get away yourself!' Swirsky shouted back. 'You old Greek shyster!'

And together they began taking down the rough planking they'd used to board up the pharmacy when Swirsky left Badminton.

I felt a bit giddy. As if I'd spent a long time on the merry-go-round and stepped off too quickly. Nobody had believed he would come back. Not even Sally who had written to him at the Leopard Rock Motel. But now he was back and it seemed no time at all had gone by. What had happened to 'for ever'?

While the men worked and we watched, the new Mrs Swirsky sat in the car. Her skin was very pale and smooth. Her hair was rich, red and full. When the sunshine touched it, it flashed flame. Now and then, she would lift one hand and flutter her finger tips at us in a feathery little wave.

'I suppose he's been around the world and I'm going to have to hear what they eat in foreign places,' said my mother when she heard about Swirsky's return.

'Fancy old Swirsky finding a wife,' my father said. 'And I'd always thought there was a touch of the nance to Nathan.'

'A touch of the what?' Each of my mother's words seemed to wear a hairy sock over it.

'Must I spell it out for you, Monica?'

My father put one hand on his hip and stood on tiptoe, waving his hand over his head. He looked like a dancing palmtree.

'For Heaven's sake, Gordon, Martin's watching you! Martin, try not to screw up your face like that. Gordon, if you don't care what ideas you put into the boy's head, at least think about passing natives.'

'I have better things to think about,' said my father, 'than passing natives.'

We could not understand why Mrs Raubenheimer and Dr Moishe, from the Jewish Old Age Home, didn't buzz around to Swirsky's pharmacy the moment he got back. My mother had been saying, ever since Swirsky left, that they were all sure to have been very good friends.

'Can they have forgotten him?' Sally asked us. 'He's been away for such a long time.'

'He's married now,' said Eric. 'They always look different when they're married.'

I was in Swirsky's pharmacy when Mrs Raubenheimer met Ruthie. I was looking at Swirsky's latest attraction. A mediaeval castle with battlements and turrets built of boxes of Sylvania 'Superflash' flash bulbs. 'Blue Dots for Sure Shots!' The moat around the castle was cut from dark blue crêpe paper and thumbtacked to the carpet.

Swirsky told Mrs Raubenheimer that Ruthie came all the way from Wimbledon, England. Mrs Raubenheimer said she believed Wimbledon was very wet.

'No wetter than anywhere else in southern England,' said Ruthie.

'Good old England,' said Swirsky. 'Where would we be without its blessed weather?'

And Mrs Raubenheimer said – 'Drizzle, drizzle, drizzle, what's so blessed about that?'

I stood in the middle of the dark blue paper moat and wondered how they could have been such friends once, as my mother believed.

When Swirsky came back so suddenly his moustache was at its best. It was a pair of black bat-wings beneath his nose. His white coats were so crisp you could almost taste them. Where the starched V of his icy lapels framed his perfect green tie you were looking at an oil painting you could eat.

His wife Ruthie, with her creamy skin and red-hot hair, was like nobody we'd ever met. She roundly spoke out all the sounds to be heard in a word and left them ringing in your ear. It was the first time we had heard English spoken by an English person and it was almost embarrassing. She talked as if she did not care who heard her. She called him Natie.

'You should travel,' he told my mother. 'I can recommend it.'

'East, West, home's best,' said my mother firmly. 'Some of us are very happy where we are, thank you.'

Swirsky bought a black motorbike and painted 'Swirsky's Pharmaceutical Supplies' in red on the white carrier box and scooted around the estate in a pair of flying goggles from his Air Force days, straps trailing in the wind.

In his first week back in the pharmacy he built the magnesia wall. A wall of dark blue bottles, six feet high stretching across his shop from nappy pins to barley sugar. The wall was a game you could see through. Bottle art. Glass painting. Looking at people through the dark blue magnesia wall turned them into glass ghosts at midnight. Soft edges and lots of depth. Afterwards it could be quite a pain to see the originals in the harsh sunlight of Henry

Street or George Crescent, bleached back to nothing interesting by the African glare, all sharp edges again, and dark tans. Just plain Mr Strydom or old Harry Hawksley or boring Gus Trupshaw.

No rains fell in Badminton for weeks and it got hotter. We knew we could expect washaways when the storms came. The water truck came twice a week and we ran behind it, barefoot, watching the fine red dust melting into mud. The stones at the roadside turned white and showed their blue veins. Ruthie Swirsky wore big straw hats and pink frocks and walked through Badminton swinging a big straw bag.

My mother said it was the first time she had seen someone wearing high heels in Henry Street. My father said that was probably how women walked out in Wimbledon. Swirsky had told him that his wife was one of the leading lights of Wimbledon. My mother said she didn't care if she was a leading light in Wimbledon. She didn't care if she was the Queen of Sheba. High heels in Henry Street was simply asking for trouble. It gave the servants ideas. What were they to think when they saw Ruthie dressed to kill? They didn't know she was from Wimbledon, did they? Who could blame them if they took a leaf from her book and began parading up and down Edward Avenue and Charles Drive. Quite enough of that sort of thing went on already. Putting on their Sunday best and walking up and down as if they owned the place.

'Have you noticed that it's on the increase, Gordon?'

'Not really,' said my father.

'You can't move for them on their days off,' said my mother. 'The women are the worst. Not two minutes ago this girl is living in a *kraal* in the veld. Next thing it's wearing high heels. A tailored suit. Lipstick, too, if you please. And the sort of hat you see at Ascot. And it's strutting along Edward Avenue like Lady Muck on toast. I wonder what Joseph Stalin would say to that? Know what I mean?'

My mother was very worried about Joseph Stalin at that time. Then the government announced that all communists were banned and my mother was very relieved. It was not a moment too soon. She did not claim to be an expert, but if you asked her, the Indians were to blame.

When Mr Govender, the travelling greengrocer, arrived in his truck, she hissed at him, 'If you think you could sell these woody tomatoes to Joseph Stalin, you've got another think coming. He'd have you shot. Thank your lucky stars that you live in the Union of South Africa and not in the Union of Soviet Socialist Republics.'

'Yes, madam,' said Mr Govender.

'Don't "yes, madam" me,' said my mother.

My father told Gus Trupshaw that Ruth Swirsky was a handsome woman. Gus Trupshaw said, yes, she was a fine looking filly. It was just a pity she was a bloody limey who went poncing about the place telling the rest of us what to do. Nathan Swirsky might find he'd bitten off more than he could chew when he took up with the Duchess of Wimbledon.

When Ruth came to tea my father told her his famous honeymoon story.

'The missus and I were on honeymoon. Down in East London. We were one short of a foursome, for a game of doubles, so I asked a bloke I met in the hotel foyer if he played. And he said, "Yes, I knock the ball about a bit." Those were his exact words, Monica will back me up. And so we get out on the court and bam, bam, bam, it's all over. Pure dynamite. Wasn't he, Monica? Anything you hit at him, you got back, with interest. But a quiet sort of chap. No airs. Thanked us nicely for the game and cleared off. Back at the hotel I'm chatting to the desk clerk and I find I've been playing tennis with Don Budge! Bloody Wimbledon champion.'

My father sent me to fetch his tennis racket and showed Ruth Swirsky the picture of Don Budge.

'I suppose you've often seen him, down your way?'

'Not everyone in Wimbledon goes to Wimbledon,' Ruthie Swirsky said.

'Don't they?' My father was amazed.

'Heavens, no,' Ruth Swirsky gave her long, strong laugh. 'We have a strong cultural tradition in Wimbledon. We've music, even pottery. And people paint. People paint in absolute droves.'

'Tennis is all we know of Wimbledon,' my mother said firmly. 'I dare say you may have had a different experience. But when you've been here a few years you'll find it's so. Say to most South Africans – "Wimbledon" – and they'll say straight back – "Tennis" – won't they Gordon?'

A few days later my mother was on the phone to Margot van Reen telling her that Ruth Swirsky had dropped in to show off her new American girdle. She had been forced to listen to that woman bragging about her Warner's 'Sta-Up-Top' girdle. And how it kept everything under control.

'What do I care about its famous won't-roll-over waistband? If that's the kind of cultural flavour they like in Wimbledon, then I feel sorry for them.'

When they came the late summer rains were heavy. Storm-water drains overflowed. The municipal dam gurgled with muddy water. Members of the Black Church of Zion baptized a lot of new members. They would gather beside the dam in white robes with blue Stars of David on their breasts and backs. A long line trailed into the water. Sally and I would watch them from the reeds on Sunday afternoons. Way out in the dam, sandy brown water right up to his waist, the priest would take a woman in his arms, and then, when it seemed that she was nice and relaxed, he'd suddenly push her under the water.

The Swirskys turned up one Sunday and watched the Black Zionists. Ruthie asked, in her clear, carrying voice that reached into the reeds, why on earth they wore Stars of David?

'It's typical of your black chappies,' said Swirsky, 'not knowing whether they're Christians or Jews.'

Ruth Swirsky clapped whenever someone was baptized and called out in her high English voice: 'Bravo!'

Later she sat on the ground with a great dripping circle of the newly baptized all around her and taught them to sing. 'I get a kick out of you!'

'It's hardly religious, I know,' she told my father when Swirsky brought her to tea one day, 'but then, that's probably just as well. They have their beliefs. I have mine. But I'm sure they loved the song. We used to dance to it at the Palais. Back home.'

'Ruthie and I sailed from Southampton,' Swirsky said. 'It's 6,008 miles from Southampton to Cape Town, as the boat plies. We came Union Castle, of course. Ruthie thought Cape Town must be rather like Nice. But she and Cape Town never really got on.'

'I liked the spectacular mule stampede,' said Ruthie, 'and the Coon Carnival was utterly fascinating. And if you want something to look at, Table Mountain is always there. But if I'm going to live in Africa, I want my Africa raw. Mind you, that doesn't mean I'm giving up my cultural side. My cultural side tells me that Badminton is ready for some good operetta.'

'And what Ruthie wants she usually gets,' Swirsky stroked his dangerous moustache.

As usual those late summer rains washed away the topsoil in the gardens that our fathers had fought to establish in the rocky veld.

The soil washed down the side of the slight hill on which Badminton stood and settled in the river.

Once again it was said that Errol the topsoil man was collecting it from the river and reselling it. Our fathers cornered Errol and demanded a reduction in the price for the rich brown loam.

'Out of the question,' Errol replied.

He'd not forgotten Reggie and when he wanted to remind everyone that he'd not forgotten Reggie, he put on Reggie's dark glasses and rode slowly down Henry Street in his truck, his elbow stuck out of the window, the sun sometimes catching his gold teeth. And on top of the pile of soil lay Reggie's wheelbarrow, upside-down, its belly mottled like an old leaf and its steel wheel slowly turning.

'God,' said my father to Gus Trupshaw down at the ex-servicemen's club, 'is a mystery. Consider. He made the world, didn't he? Well, then, a child could have told him that if you allow slippery creatures to prosper, you end up with an Errol selling topsoil twice over.'

I studied the new paper cloths on the table. That month they were supplied by courtesy of Castle Beer and carried a toast from a man with a checked suit, handlebar moustache and thick glasses. He held a glass of beer and said: 'Your Health Sir . . .' This was the world-famous BBC commentator Raymond Glendenning. His smile showed his big square teeth. There were gaps between his teeth. His moustache was ragged. Not at all like Swirsky's sharp black needles.

Gus Trupshaw said to my father, 'So you think that your Asian is the slipperiest businessman you ever saw? Your Syrian outdoes him every time.'

'That so, Gus?' My father raised his eyebrows in the polite way that meant he did not think so.

'Believe me, Gordon.' Gus Trupshaw lit a cigarette and

flicked a match across the room, so hard that it pinged off the light-bulb in the middle of the room. Gus Trupshaw could fire a match through a wall of newspaper, three sheets thick. He'd learnt to do it in the Army.

'I was in Damascus, you know, before the balloon went up.'

'So you were, Gus,' my father said, 'so you were.'

About this time Eric ran away again. We heard about it later from Swirsky. His mother, who was already late for tennis, was called to the Comet Tea Room in Cyrildene and found Eric sitting under the pinball table, almost lost among the legs of the men playing.

'I'm waiting to tell God about Sammie.'

'Don't tilt the table, son,' the players shouted in the Comet Tea Room as Eric ran for the door.

'I'll give you God!' said his ma, and chased him with her tennis racquet.

Eric had the marks of his mother's gut strings on his legs and arms where she had struck him with her Slazenger. He got out of his ma's car and ran to the pharmacy and hid behind Swirsky's counter and he wouldn't come out until Swirsky tempted him with an empty plastic nasal-spray bottle. It made a fine water pistol.

When Sally, Tony and I arrived at Swirsky's pharmacy, Eric and Swirsky were having a water fight out in the backyard. Eric was behind the loquat tree and he hit Swirsky straight in the chest.

Swirsky crumbled very slowly and put his hand on Sally's shoulder. 'Pesky Redskins got me, podner,' he groaned. 'Tell Maw her boy Nathan died with his boots on.'

Then he sank to the ground and lay so still that only his moustache moved when the wind blew.

Sally said, 'Come on, Mr Swirsky, get up.' But Swirsky lay there so still she shook him. 'Please, Mr Swirsky . . .' and her voice shook like her hand. 'We know you're only bluffing.'

Sally lifted one leg and crossed it over the other and laced the toes of her right foot into the toes of her left foot. She pulled out her blue Alice band, shook her blonde hair in the sunshine and slipped the Alice band back into place. She was so quick and neat. Everything about her fitted together.

Swirsky opened one eye. 'A miracle,' he said.

Ruth Swirsky walked on to the lawn. 'Natie, you're sopping wet. And your tie's ruined.' Her high heels made holes in the grass. 'Sometimes I think you're a great big child.'

Tony started hopping from foot to foot when he saw Ruth Swirsky, grabbing at the front of his shorts. 'It wasn't us that did it, Mrs Swirsky.'

'You banana,' said his sister.

Eric shinned up the loquat tree and vanished among its dark green leaves.

Swirsky got to his feet and looked down at his tie, tapping it with his chin, at the same time pushing up his lower lip until it touched his moustache. His white coat was soaking. Through it I could see his braces.

'No harm done, sweetie,' he said. 'The African sun will dry me out in two ticks.'

'You've got a lot of faith in the blessed African sun,' said Ruthie. 'I want you right on the night, Nathan Swirsky. Come inside and change those clothes.'

She walked back into the shop, her high heels stab-stabbing the grass. Swirsky trailed along, waddling as he always did, with his toes pointing outward, and a grassy smear, showing he had lain down on the lawn, running like a green road between his braces.

We called him but Eric refused to come down from the tree. He just rustled a little in the leaves above our heads. So we left him there and walked home, with Tony saying again and again, 'Well, I didn't know he was going to climb into the tree, did I?'

Sally took the tennis ball from her pocket and shoved it down the front of her dress. She bulged hugely, in a lop-sided way.

'You're not allowed to do that,' Tony said, 'Mom says it's rude.'

Sally stuck out her big left chest and marched down Henry Street swinging her arms, as if she didn't care who saw her.

'I'll tell,' her brother warned her.

Sally took the ball out of her chest, bowled a good looping leg-break against a telephone pole, and hit it plumb centre. She was the best bowler on the estate. She was also very clever with knots.

'Wait till it's dark, and Eric still is not home,' she said. 'His ma's going to murder someone. Don't you think Eric's ma's going to murder someone, Martin?'

'Says who?' Tony wanted to know.

Sally lifted her nose and wouldn't answer him. Tony turned white around his lips and suddenly he ran off down the street and into his yard.

'He'll go and hide under his bed now.' Sally put her tennis ball back in her pocket. 'For about three hours. He's a great big child.' And we laughed because she sounded just like Ruthie Swirsky.

In bed that night I knew that Sally was right about Tony. But Ruthie had been wrong about Swirsky. He was not a child. He had a moustache like the world-famous BBC commentator, Raymond Glendenning. Except Swirsky's moustache was better.

It was sharp and shapely. It was as neat as a pick-axe head. And Swirsky did not have the teeth of the BBC man with the beer glass. Old teeth. Before I fell asleep, I thought – yes – that was it. Swirsky was grown-up but he was not grown-old. I hoped he would be right on the night – as Ruth Swirsky had said. Though I could not think what that night would be.

We were sitting on top of Errol's pile of soil when Ruthie Swirsky waved at us as we rode past her shop.

'I say, Mr Topsoil Man,' called Ruthie Swirsky, 'I'd like three loads of dressing please. For my new lawn.'

She had dug up all the grass under the loquat tree. She had sown new grass plants. 'Nathan was prepared to settle for native Kikuyu grass. I want a real lawn.'

Errol said, 'Sure thing, ma'am,' and shovelled topsoil across the fence.

'Do you always work alone, Mr Topsoil Man?'

Errol pulled at the collar of his white shirt in the nervous way he had. Then, still standing with one foot on her fence and the other on the side of his truck, he told her about Reggie.

Ruthie said, 'You poor, poor man. How ghastly. And you never found him again?'

She went inside and came out with a cup of tea and a jam sandwich. 'How absolutely frightful!' she said in her carrying voice.

Gus Trupshaw who was passing asked what the trouble was.

'This man lost his little friend. And has never found him again.'

'These things happen,' said Gus Trupshaw.

'It's heart-breaking.'

'I wouldn't exactly go that far,' said Gus Trupshaw.

'I would,' said Ruthie Swirsky. 'You can be sure. I shall keep my eye open for this little pink missing boy, wherever I go.'

She paid Errol for the topsoil and did not complain about the price.

Gus Trupshaw tried to tell her what the others thought by saying, 'Friend Errol doesn't do too badly. With or without his missing partner. Believe me, Ruth, he really does rather well.'

'So he should,' said Ruth Swirsky. 'He's earned it, hasn't he?'

'Thanks, missus,' said Errol and threw his shovel with a clatter on to the back of his truck.

'The madam wasn't talking to you,' said Gus Trupshaw.

As he pulled himself into his cab Ruthie suddenly asked Errol if he rented out his truck.

Errol looked surprised. 'Try anything once, madam.'

'You can say that again,' said Gus Trupshaw.

'Good-oh.' Ruth Swirsky smiled straight at Errol so that Gus Trupshaw would know who she was talking to.

A few days later posters were to be seen in the window of Swirsky's pharmacy, and in the Greek Tea Room and down at Mr Benjamin, the Rug Doctor's:

The Merry Widow
3 Performances
Proceeds in Aid of the South African National TB
    Association.
Come One – Come All!

My mother said: 'Doesn't Ruth Swirsky realize she's a million miles from Wimbledon?'

I knew what she meant but I also knew that a million miles from Wimbledon was closer to somewhere than we were to anywhere.

For several days Errol drove his truck slowly down Henry Street, Charles Drive, Elizabeth Crescent and Edward Avenue with a big cardboard display on the back:

> *Love, Laughter, Music*
> *Meet the Merry Widow*
> *In the Kindergarten Hall*

The letters were cut from the blue crêpe paper that Swirsky had used for his mediaeval castle moat. Every so often Errol tooted his horn and gave the thumbs up. He wore Reggie's dark glasses.

My mother shook her head. 'She really thinks because she's in South Africa, she can do as she likes. If she was in Russia Stalin would soon put a stop to that.'

Everyone turned up at the first night. Ladies from the Jewish home came, dressed in silk and wonderfully perfumed. Our fathers wore their Army demob suits, wide straight trousers and rumpled lapels. They had their hair freshly cut and showed shaved necks and boney spaces above their ears. They smelt of shaving cream and Vaseline hair oil. They teased Gus Trupshaw who was the only one to wear his medals. My father said it felt too much like a church parade. And Eric's father sang 'Tarara Boompsiay/I want a holiday . . .' which, he said, was the only opera he knew.

Swirsky was wearing white tie and tails. He said, 'Hullo, Martin, how do you like my penguin outfit?' And he held out his hand and told me to shake his flipper. 'Ruthie met this singing troupe on the boat when we sailed from Southampton. Being cultural, Ruthie and these operetta types got on like houses on fire. *The Merry Widow*'s an operetta, remember that chaps. Call it opera and Ruthie will have your guts for garters. Ruthie isn't sure Badminton's ready for grand opera yet.'

Ruthie Swirsky was wearing a long pink dress and long white gloves which she kept pushing up over her elbows. She jabbed an elbow towards the entrance where our fathers were standing about among the pictures the kindergarten kids had stuck on the walls. 'Gus Trupshaw has already been asking about the bar. I don't want the men starting on the beer before the interval.'

'Leave it to me, sweetie,' Swirsky said. 'I told you everything would be fine on the night.'

From the moment the tall blond baritone and the little widow, dark and plump, stepped on to the stage and started singing in German you could feel the chill.

'Jeez, Gus,' said my father as he and Gus Trupshaw pulled at bottles of lager during the interval and flicked cigarette ash into the rose bushes. 'It seems just the other day that Jerry was pounding the hell out of us at El Alamein. Now we're paying good money to have him do it again.'

Gus Trupshaw shook his head until the medals on his chest rang. They said it all for him. They said: 'You can bloody well say that again, Gordon!'

My father said that Eric's father had been a POW in Germany. 'Came home as thin as a bloody coathanger. Look at him now.'

Gus Trupshaw said he was going to call a meeting of the Torch Commando. The 'Torchies' would teach the Germans you couldn't mess around with Desert Rats. Rommel had found that out in the war up North.

And when we all trailed back into the hall after the interval, the ladies from the Jewish Old Age Home had disappeared and there were rows of empty seats.

The next morning it was all over the estate. The Jewish Old Age Home had asked the Swirskys to close down the German opera.

Sally had been behind the magnesia wall and heard Mrs

Raubenheimer saying, 'We won't have it, Mr Swirsky.'

'It's a light-hearted operetta,' Swirsky said.

Ruth Swirsky said, 'The war's been over for nearly ten years.'

'And anyway, the troupe's not German,' Swirsky said. 'They're Austrian.'

'So was Hitler,' said Mrs Raubenheimer. 'And so were lots of his troops.'

When she'd gone Ruthie said: 'It's the principle of the thing.'

'Absolutely, sweetie,' said her husband.

Sally watched Ruthie walk up and down a couple of times. Then she climbed the ladder to the highest shelves in the shop and sat on the top rung with her chin in her hands. She was sitting directly between the Benefax Tablets which helped undersized children to grow taller and which Sammie's ma had fed him for years without helping him at all, and a model of the Eiffel Tower Swirsky had built from bottles of blood purifier. Then Ruthie got down off the ladder and walked over to Sally who thought no one could see her behind the magnesia wall.

'Run me an errand, little girl,' she said. 'Find Errol the topsoil man and tell him I have another job for his truck.'

It took Errol three trips to get all the Black Zionists, whistling and waving from the back of his truck, to the kindergarten hall. They filled just about every seat on the second night.

Swirsky handed us free tickets. 'It's called papering the house. All the smart musical promoters do it. As you'll find, when you visit La Scala or Carnegie Hall.'

When Ruthie came out in front of the curtain before the show started, wearing her pink gown and her long white gloves, the Zionists clapped. Then they gave her a burst of 'I Get A Kick Out Of You'.

'Very wonderful,' she touched her gloves to her lips and blew them kisses. 'Thank you, one and all. But remember – once the curtain goes up, the only singing I want to hear comes from the stage.'

When the curtain came down we all clapped like mad. Ruthie Swirsky came to us, still clapping.

'Won't you help me say goodbye, and thank you, to these glorious singers? It's not their fault they're Austrian – is it?'

We went backstage and Mrs Swirsky introduced us to the little dark widow. And the big blond baritone.

'This is Mr Christ,' Ruthie said. And when she saw Sally smile, she said: 'It's quite a common Austrian name, children.'

The blond man leaned down and kissed her hand. 'How can someone so beautiful look so sad?'

Ruthie smiled. 'Thank you for a thrilling evening. You sang like a god. If I may say so. Bravo!'

'Bravo!' shouted the Black Church of Zion who were waiting outside the hall. Tony whispered that it was the same at rugby matches. Black people always cheered for the overseas team. Then the singers climbed into their Volkswagen minivan, and, with Ruthie leading the way, we all waved goodbye.

MAUNDY

A FEW days before Easter, Maggie's father found a man in a sanitary lane, and took him home. All over Badminton sandy, stony sanitary lanes ran between the houses on Edward Avenue and Henry Street and Elizabeth Crescent. They had been built so that the night-soil men, coming like ghosts after dark, could remove the black rubber buckets without being seen.

Nobody talked about the night-soil men. They came and went in our sleep, though in the morning we caught the scent of something we wished to forget.

Nobody talked about Maggie, either, even though she lived next door, took off all her clothes from time to time and ran around her house. And we all pretended not to notice. She was the fastest ten-year-old on the estate.

My mother was next door in a flash when she saw the man working in Maggie's garden. He wore old khaki shorts. His legs ended in stumps, inches below the shorts, and the stumps were tied up in sacking. He pulled himself everywhere in a red tin wagon, hauling himself along with strong arms. His muscles were huge. The legless man sat upon a paper bag that he had spread in the bottom of his wagon. Later I saw that it read: *Buy Your Brand-New Zephyr At Dominion Motors.*

'Hell's bells! What could I do? He just followed me home,'

said Maggie's father. 'He tells me his name's Salisbury.'

'I don't care if he's the King of Siam,' my mother said to my father a little while later. 'It's bad enough when that little girl tears about the place in the you-know-what, for all the world and his wife to stare. Now they have a cripple in their garden!'

My father was studying the annual report of the South African Sugar Association. 'Figures for 1953 show exports up.'

'Some of us cannot lose ourselves in sugar reports,' my mother said. 'Some of us have to look life in the eye.'

'For Heaven's sake, Monica,' my father said, 'the poor sod's lost his legs. I'm sure he doesn't like it any more than you do. But he's still human. Well, more or less.'

Then Maggie appeared, running around the side of her house. 'Speak of the devil!' my mother said. Maggie was skinny and very brown. Her bare legs flashing, round and round the house she ran. Her dog, a Dobermann called Tamburlaine, ran after her, barking loudly.

'Martin,' said my mother, 'come away from the window. It only encourages her if you stare.'

Maggie's father was chasing her with a blanket. He caught up, and threw it over her. Like a big grey butterfly net.

'You'd hardly think this was Easter,' said my mother. 'I don't know where to put my face.'

Salisbury sat in his red wagon, doing some weeding. 'What on earth do you think is going through his head?' my mother demanded. 'That little girl might be less keen to parade in the altogether if she knew what was going through his head.'

'I see that Henry's been planting out beardless irises,' said my father. 'The beardless iris loves a sunny spot and a good bit of wall.'

'Heavens above, where will it all end?' my mother asked. 'Our neighbours have a cripple in their garden. Easter is almost on us. There are burglars in the bluegums. Soon the streets will be full of servants. Did you know that they've taken to asking for Easter boxes? First Christmas boxes, now Easter boxes. I suppose they'll be asking for Michaelmas boxes next. Dressed to the nines, some of them. And worse for wear.'

I went to bed that night and thought about the burglars down among the bluegums. All over Badminton our fathers slept with their Army-issue pistols in their sock drawers, ready at any moment to rush naked into the African night, blasting away. The burglars were said to creep up on the houses and cast fishing lines through the anti-burglar bars to hook wallets and handbags from our bedrooms.

We all believed in the burglars. Everyone except for Ruthie Swirsky, the chemist's new wife. But she was English, from Wimbledon. 'Burglars with fishing rods,' Ruthie Swirsky said to my father just after she moved to the Estate. 'I've never heard of anything so absurd. Pull the other one, Gordon.'

'Pull the other what?' my mother wanted to know later.

'How would I know, Monica?' said my father. 'Leg, I suppose.'

'Whatever she had in mind, it wasn't a leg,' said my mother.

'Whatever she had in mind, it wasn't a leg!' sang my friends Tony, Sally and Eric, and I as we rolled down the steep, grassy banks in Tony's garden that Easter time in Badminton.

For the rest of the holiday, nothing much seemed likely to happen. The days looming ahead were too hot somehow, even though we were well into autumn. Our fathers tended to their petunias and phlox and chrysanthemums. They sprayed their rosebushes against black spot, moving in the thick clouds of lime and sulphur like refugees from a gas attack in the trenches.

Ernest Langbein had fallen in love with Maggie. Ernest was an altar server at the Church of the Resurrection in Cyrildene, and he told Eric that if only Maggie would stop taking off her clothes, their love might be possible. Maggie was not easy to get on with. When she had no clothes on, she wasn't really there. And when she was dressed she was inclined to make savage remarks. I met her in Swirsky's Pharmacy on Maundy Thursday. She wore a blue dress with thick black stockings. Her brown, pixie face was shaded by a big white panama hat, tied beneath her chin with thick elastic. I was wearing shorts. I'd never seen her look so covered up. She looked at my bare feet and said, 'You have hammertoes, Martin.' It seemed very unfair.

We were standing behind the wall of blue magnesia bottles which Swirsky had built across his shop. We heard Ruthie Swirsky say to Mrs Raubenheimer, 'I'm collecting Maundy money. It's an Easter custom we have in England. The Royal Mint makes its own money, and the Queen gives it to pensioners and suchlike. The deserving poor. In a special purse.'

Mrs Raubenheimer said that those who could afford it could afford it. Swirsky crackled as he rounded the magnesia wall and grinned at us. His moustache was full and yet feathery beneath his nose. Black feathers, it was. 'Well, kiddies,' he said. 'Can I count on you? Pocket money is welcome for Ruthie's Maundy box. What Ruthie wants she usually gets.' He rattled a black wooden collection box.

My mother said, 'It's appalling. The Swirskys aren't even Easter people. The Queen of England does not live on an estate infested with burglars. Have you seen the collection box Ruthie Swirsky's using? I happen to know that it belongs to St John's Ambulance. She simply turned it around so you can't see the badge.'

'If you're going to divide the world into those who are and those who are not Easter people,' said my father, 'you may as well go and join the government. They do it all the time.'

'I have no intention,' said my mother, 'of joining the government.'

All the kids gave to Ruthie Swirsky's Maundy-money box. We collected empty soft-drink bottles and got back a penny deposit down at the Greek Tea Room. Swirsky shook the box until our pennies rattled. 'Give till it hurts,' he said. 'Baby needs new booties.'

A deputation arrived at the pharmacy. Gus Trupshaw had been elected to speak for the Estate. He wore his demob suit and brown Army boots with well-polished toes. He said that everyone objected to the idea of Ruthie giving away money to the servants. What would they expect next Easter? It might be difficult for an English person to understand. But the cleaners, cooks and gardeners of Badminton got board and lodging and wages. 'They might be poor,' Gus Trupshaw explained, 'but they're not deserving.'

'Are you telling me I may not give my Maundy money to whomsoever I choose?' Ruthie asked, with her face white beneath her red hair. 'This is outrageous.'

'This isn't Wimbledon,' said Gus Trupshaw. 'When in Rome, do as the Romans do.'

Swirsky leaned over to us and whispered. 'When you're next in Rome, I can recommend the Trevi Fountain. But watch out for pickpockets.'

Ruthie Swirsky tapped the black collection box with her finger after Gus Trupshaw left. She told Swirsky she was so mad she could spit. She asked him to find Errol the topsoil man. 'Tell him I have a job for his wheelbarrow.'

Later, it was my mother who spotted Errol wheeling his

barrow into the yard next door. 'There appears to be some movement at the neighbours'. I think I'll go and lie down,' she said.

Errol stopped beside Salisbury with his wheelbarrow. He laid
the paper bag from Dominion Motors on the floor of the barrow
and lifted Salisbury out of his wagon. Then he set off up Henry
Street, wheeling Salisbury, with Sally, Tony, Eric and me tagging
along behind them.

We heard the iron wheels scattering gravel in Henry Street.

'Where are we going?' Salisbury asked Errol in a deep,
growling voice.

'Boss Swirsky's place. Sit still and don't make trouble.' Errol
manoeuvred the barrow right up to the front door of Swirsky's
Pharmacy. Papas, the owner of the Greek Tea Room, and Mr
Benjamin, the Rug Doctor, came out of their shops to stare. A
couple of ladies from the Jewish Old Age Home also stopped to
watch. Ruthie Swirsky came out of the pharmacy. Nathan was
next to her. There was sun on his moustache, and it looked as if
it had been dipped in oil. Swirsky carried the collection box. He
held it carefully, as if it were a baby, and his face when he looked
at Ruthie was soft and loving. A crowd of cleaners, cooks and
gardeners gathered across the road. They were shouting things.

'I hear you're a poor man, Salisbury,' said Ruthie. 'So I've
decided to help you.'

'Yes, madam,' said Salisbury.

'I hope you're not going to leave him there all day, Mrs
Swirsky,' said Mrs Raubenheimer.

Ruthie ignored everyone. 'This box is yours. Take it home
with you. Take it back to your family. Take it with my blessings.'

'Yes, madam,' said Salisbury.

Errol wheeled him home quickly. Salisbury held the box
tight to his chest. All over the estate there were servants watching.
You could tell the servants were angry because they weren't

allowed to have any of the Maundy money. Some of them shouted at Errol as he wheeled Salisbury down Henry Street.

'That's what you get from Africans and Asians!' said my mother. 'That's exactly the sort of thing that led to the Cato Manor Riots. We could be facing more of them. Mark my words.'

Later that night, we were woken by people shouting next door. Tamburlaine the Dobermann began barking. Someone was crying. My father got up and put on his brown woollen dressing gown. 'Take your hockey stick, Gordon,' said my mother. To me she said, 'Martin, you take the torch, I'm going to call the police.'

We found Maggie and her father trying to lift Salisbury into his red wagon. He was crying and swearing and waving his strong arms about.

'He's as strong as a lion, Gordon,' said Maggie's father. 'Help me. I think Tamburlaine's taken a nip out of him.'

Then Gus Trupshaw arrived and fired several shots. He thought he was using his starting pistol, but he'd grabbed a flare gun by mistake and the sky was like noon for minutes. I could see Salisbury's tears.

'He says somebody has stolen his money,' said Maggie's father. 'People came and robbed him. I let him sleep here last night. I gave him the toolshed to doss down in. In the morning Errol was going to wheel him to the bus stop. He was going home.'

Salisbury sat in the red tin wagon, rubbing his eyes and crying.

'Lock him in the toolshed,' my father suggested. 'Anything to keep him away from that dog. We'll sort this out in the morning.'

'It's very hard,' said Gus Trupshaw. 'We'll have to replace the money. We'll have a whip round. I just hope Ruthie Swirsky knows what she's done. You can't mess around with Africa.'

But they had reckoned without Salisbury's strong arms.

When they went to the toolshed in the morning, Salisbury was gone. He had torn the door off its hinges. He had levered himself into his little red wagon, and he had vanished.

'Thank Heavens for small mercies,' said my mother.

On Thursday afternoon, Errol found the little tin wagon down by the bluegums. Then a party of men found Salisbury. He was hanging from a branch by his belt. The men made a kind of tent of blankets around him, so that the children shouldn't see.

Ruthie Swirsky waited for the police to come and take Salisbury away. She asked the constable if she might send a little something to his next of kin. The constable laughed at her and said, 'People like Salisbury have no next of kin.' Ruthie Swirsky asked the constable for his number. And he threatened to arrest her.

The police took Salisbury away, and it might have ended there. Except that Ruthie Swirsky found out that he had a brother and a sister in a village sixty miles away. 'This is ridiculous!' said Gus Trupshaw. 'If we had to take responsibility for every soul that dies, where would we be?'

On Easter Saturday, the coffin turned up on the back of Errol the topsoil man's truck. 'Mrs Swirsky, she arranged it,' said Errol.

'She actually believes she's still in Wimbledon,' said my father. But he and Gus Trupshaw offered to drive the coffin back to Salisbury's home village. We all watched as they loaded it on to the back of Gus Trupshaw's new Ford truck. 'If you don't hear from us in a week, send a search party,' said Gus Trupshaw.

'For Heaven's sake,' said my mother. 'You're only driving to the other side of Rustenberg. Just explain that you're very sorry about what happened, and don't tell them where you live.'

The men got home at sunset. 'We would've been back earlier,' my father said, grinning. 'But we had a feast with the family. It's tradition. They wanted to thank us for bringing him home.'

'Chicken and rice,' said Gus Trupshaw.

'Quite normal, really,' said my father.

'Normal? My godfathers, Gordon,' said my mother. 'It may be normal to you. But I was worried sick. And there are Easter eggs to be hidden in our garden tonight. The children have waited up while you've been eating chicken and rice.'

You could tell that the men were pleased with themselves. It was as if they had been through some huge adventure at the other end of the world.

'Yes,' said Gus Trupshaw, as though they did such things every day. 'First chicken and rice. And then peaches.'

They came into the kitchen and my mother said to me, 'Your father's been eating chicken, with strangers.'

'Quite normal, really,' said my father again.

My mother held up a hand. 'Please. Not another word. It gives me the heebie-jeebies just thinking about it.'

We were sitting around the house waiting to be sent to bed as soon as our fathers were ready to hide the Easter eggs. They always hid them the night before. And we were always sent to bed. It was often far too early for bed, sometimes the sunset was still playing on the curtains and I would lie there feeling idiotic. My mother would call out, asking if my face was turned to the wall. Just as she did when the Torch Commando were out on a secret raid. My mother said that the Easter Bunny would not come, if I was not asleep. There wasn't a single eleven-year-old in Badminton who believed in the Easter Bunny. Except maybe my mother. And I didn't enjoy the Easter egg hunt. Everyone shouted when I set off in the wrong direction.

'Why do dogs only bite black people?' Tony asked.

'They don't. Last year, our Aunt Mary got bitten – didn't she? And she's from Kenya,' said Sally. 'Do you know anyone not black who has been bitten, Martin?' Sally wore a dress the colour of apricots. Her shiny yellow hair was held tightly in a blue Alice band. Her brown legs were bare. She had this habit of feeding the toes of one foot into the other.

I said, 'I remember Strydom's dog, Attila, bit the postman once.'

'Martin will say anything. Just to please you,' Tony loudly snapped the elastic in the waistband of his brown boxer shorts. 'Because Martin adores you.'

'Rubbish!' said Sally. 'You don't really adore me, do you, Mart?'

'I don't adore anyone,' I said.

'Oh yes, Mart – then why are you blushing?' Maggie asked.

Swirsky arrived on his motorbike with Papas sitting in the sidecar. Papas carried a big cardboard box with *Sundowner Brandy* written on it. We knew that the box held our Easter eggs, which Papas got wholesale from his cousin in Orange Grove. One Easter, Gus Trupshaw had said he could get eggs much cheaper through a connection in Fordsburg. But my father said Papas would not stand for that. Greeks were very big on Easter.

Other fathers began arriving. They made a barbecue and stood around the fire, watching the meat sizzling on the old garden sieve my father used for a grill. They drank beer. By about eight o'clock, Papas was singing 'She'll be comin' round the mountain when she comes'. My mother stuck her head out of the kitchen window and said, 'Excuse me! May I remind you that there are children present.'

Gus Trupshaw called back, 'Aye, aye, Captain.'

*

Later, for what seemed like hours, I lay in my dark bedroom listening to the men yelling to each other. I heard my father saying, 'Go left, Gus, further left! Dead on target now. That's beautiful.' Then Papas would call out, 'Am I on course, Gordon?' And my father would shout back, 'You're at two o'clock, George. Beautiful. Steady as she goes.'

Much later, I grew sleepy and it seemed to me that the men in the garden were not men at all. They were planes and tanks moving across the sand in the desert war in North Africa. While, in the yard next door, Tamburlaine keened and whimpered. His long chain, which had been tied to the steel pole that held the washing line, clashed like the waves of a metal sea.

On Easter morning, we were out in the garden soon after breakfast. We had gone to bed too early. Then we got up too early – so we could hunt for the chocolate eggs before the sun melted them. Our fathers stood blinking in the early morning sunshine, rubbing their eyes and yawning. They had not had time to shave. Mr Strydom brought Precious who gave his gummy smile and galloped on the spot.

'Servants on an Easter egg hunt?' My mother hissed at my father. 'They'll soon be sitting down to supper with us.'

Mr Swirsky brought Ruthie to watch her very first African Easter egg hunt. She told my mother she would never get used to Easter in autumn. South Africa was all upside-down. My mother told her to hang on to her hat. She'd been living in South Africa all her life, and there was lots she still was not used to. Swirsky smoothed his moustache with a small, soft white hand. He seemed to be stroking the wings of a special bird. Ruthie wore sunglasses. With her red hair and pale skin, and huge dark glass eyes, she seemed very mysterious.

'She looks like an English spy,' Tony whispered.

'No chit-chat in the ranks,' my father ordered.

'Ruthie has sensitive eyes,' Swirsky told everyone. 'Those glasses were specially shipped all the way from England. I kid you not.'

One by one, we set off, slowly, like blind people, to find our eggs while the men shouted clues. 'You're ice-cold, Martin! Your right foot's a bit warmer now. Which one is your right foot? Now your knee is getting rather warm. Oh, Martin, your knee is on fire. Can't you feel the heat, boy?'

Swirsky got carried away and tried to take over from my father. He kept shouting out, 'Two o'clock, Martin. Angels at two o'clock!'

When we had found our chocolate eggs, it was Precious' turn. My mother wanted to make him wear gloves, remembering the time when people thought he was a leper. But my father said he was using his hands in the garden and the roses were not likely to catch something – were they?

'We try to treat our servants as part of the family,' my father told Ruth Swirsky. 'At Christmas and Easter, the servants are always included. We don't have to do it. We choose to do it.'

Precious fell on his knees and clapped his hands when Mr Strydom pointed to the garden.

My mother explained quietly to Ruthie Swirsky, 'He's a bit touched in the head. Easter must be a real puzzle. Their customs are very different from ours. But I suppose that's something you well understand.'

'You mean, being British?' Ruthie asked.

'Well, that too,' said my mother.

Precious did not understand the 'hot' and 'cold' directions. He danced about the garden as if he were hunting game. His ears were pricked; his hands were held in little paws in front of his chest. He was very springy on his feet, making little leaps this way and that. He danced across to the rockery. The men shouted: 'You're cold, cold, Precious!' Then he went the other way, and they shouted, 'You're warm, warmer, Precious!' But Precious didn't listen to them. He went back to the rockery and fell on his knees, and my father said, 'Oh God, not another praying session.'

And my mother called out, 'Language, Gordon. This is Easter Sunday.'

When Precious got to his feet, he had found something. But it wasn't wrapped in silver paper like the other eggs. It was square and black. Gus Trupshaw said, 'Now, what the hell have you got there, boy?'

Precious ran over to him like a retriever and dropped his prize at his feet.

'That's my Maundy money-box,' Ruthie said. 'Give it to me, Precious.' She reached out her hands for it. But Precious fell on his knees again, smiling hugely and happily, and hugged the black wooden box to his chest.

'Thank you, God!' said Precious.

'Hell's bells!' I heard my father say. 'This could be tricky.'

Ruthie said, in her clear English voice, 'But this is absurd! Someone make him give me my box.'

'Finders keepers,' Gus Trupshaw said. 'Precious thinks it was meant for him.'

'But it doesn't belong to him,' Ruthie said. 'Somebody stole that box from Salisbury. They must have hidden it in your garden. Salisbury did away with himself because he thought he'd never see that money again. And all the time it was a few feet away.' And she began crying.

Mr Strydom promised to try and make Precious give up the box. But he didn't sound too sure about it.

Swirsky said, 'Don't, sweetie. I'll fix it.' But from the sound of his voice we knew that there was nothing much to be done.

141

'Strictly speaking,' my mother said, when the Swirskys had left, 'that box belongs to St John's Ambulance. It wasn't hers to give away in the first place.'

Precious took the black wooden box next door. Before disappearing inside, he held up the box like a football captain hoists a prize-winning cup above his head. 'Precious is happy,' he told us.

Nobody else was happy. The cooks and cleaners and gardeners from Badminton Estate took to stopping outside the Strydoms' fence and staring. Someone shouted. A stone was thrown. Precious watched from behind the kitchen window. Genghis the giant man-eater snarled at black passersby. But he wasn't really much good to Precious. Mr Strydom told everyone he was sleeping with his revolver under his pillow. But that wasn't much good to Precious either. He sat behind the kitchen window clutching his black box to his chest like a prisoner in a cage.

A few days later Gus Trupshaw announced that his maid and several other women, washing clothes down by the bluegums, had been frightened by a vision of Salisbury. Salisbury wore the belt that he'd used to hang himself. He had come back to haunt them, floating above the ground, skimming along the gravel, belt flying from his neck. He had chased the women all the way up Edward Avenue.

'Flying ghosts at Easter!' my mother said. 'What will they think of next? I only hope Ruth Swirsky realizes what she's done. Once they get an idea like this into their heads, they don't let go. We'll have the police here. Mark my words.'

We were hanging over the Strydoms' fence when Swirsky turned up at Strydom's house and asked to see Precious. Swirsky wore a stethoscope and his wife's dark glasses. His chemist's coat was as smooth as an envelope. Mr Strydom told him that Precious had locked himself in the bathroom because people were threatening to kill him.

'I intend to fight fire with fire,' said Swirsky.

He came out of the house a long time later in his shirt sleeves. Precious was with him. In Swirsky's pale face his moustache was so black it might have been drawn with charcoal. Precious wore Swirsky's white chemist's coat. He wore Ruthie Swirsky's dark glasses and the stethoscope was slung around his neck. Precious put the stethoscope to his chest and listened to his heart. 'Boum, boum, boum,' he said proudly.

My mother had been waiting. She strode to the fence. Swirsky carried the St John's Ambulance box. 'Fair exchange, no robbery. But he drives a hard bargain, does Precious. Given half a chance, he could run the ruddy country.'

'Would you please keep your voice down?' my mother asked, smiling, and speaking without moving her lips.

Later that afternoon, Sally came round to my place and said that there was a religious meeting in the bluegums. We ran down the hill to the little frothing river in the thick bank of enormous trees. Errol the topsoil man was there. Gus Trupshaw stopped in his new truck. 'Is this a church parade?' he asked. 'Where's the bally sky pilot?' A crowd of servants waited under the bluegums. Swirsky and his wife arrived in his dark green Opel. From the back of the car stepped a tall black woman in a red skirt. She was barefoot. She wore great bracelets of beads around her wrists. There were chicken bladders in her hair, like little yellow balloons. There were rows of beads crossed over her chest.

Ruthie Swirsky held up her hand for silence. 'This is Ethel,' she pointed to the tall woman. 'Ethel is a *Sangoma*. A witch doctor.'

Ethel knelt on the ground. She untied a leather bag that was hanging from her waist. She opened the bag and put it on the ground in front of her. Then she closed her eyes and seemed to go to sleep. With her eyes closed, she tipped some bones from the bag into her palms and blew on them – a long loud breath. She threw them in the dirt as if she were throwing dice. Then she opened her eyes and studied the bones. Next she took from under her arm the wooden St John's Ambulance box. Swirsky stepped forward, pulling Salisbury's red wagon. The crowd groaned and shivered when they saw that it still carried the brown paper with which Salisbury had lined his wagon: *Buy Your Brand-New Zephyr At Dominion Motors*. Ethel shook the collection box. We heard our pennies and sixpences rattling inside. People began clapping softly. Ethel produced a bottle of petrol and a box of matches. In a moment, the box was blazing in the red wagon. No one said a word. We watched until nothing was left but a smell of paint from the red wagon, ashes, and a pile of glowing, smoking coins.

Ethel leaned over and stirred the money to cool it. Everybody was given a piece of money, black from the fire. I got a sixpence. Sally received a shilling. Even Errol the topsoil man got a florin. Examining the scorched money, Swirsky said, 'King George doesn't look too pleased – he's got a black eye.'

Sally said, 'It's like getting coins out of a Christmas pudding.'

Then Ethel, the witch doctor, stepped back into the Opel.

'I was very moved,' Ruthie Swirsky told her.

Ethel lit a Mills cigarette and blew smoke at the roof of the car. 'You're welcome,' said Ethel.

'Will Salisbury be happy, Mr Swirsky?' Eric asked.

'We had to make contact,' Swirsky said. 'That's Ethel's real forte. Making contact. Apparently, the wandering spirit needs some form of direction. This way or that? It's a bit like looking for Easter eggs. Colder? Or warmer? We made a special fire so the spirit of Salisbury could warm itself.'

'And the Maundy money I collected was given to the deserving poor. If I'd been allowed to do that in the first place, none of this would have happened,' said Ruthie Swirsky.

My mother said, when I showed her my blackened sixpence, 'Don't try and spend it, Martin. Scorched coins are not legal tender. Ask your father.'

CHUMS

THE trouble started when Swirsky told Mrs Raubenheimer of the Jewish Old Age Home that his new wife had been 'raised' in Wimbledon. My mother heard this from Gus Trupshaw. Her lips tightened and she said that we had not exactly been dragged up in Badminton, thank you very much. And South Africa was a perfectly good place in spite of Nathan Swirsky's ballyhoo about England. Gus Trupshaw said that Swirsky was also making a song and dance about his new French perfumes. His shop ponged like a Cairo cathouse. My father said Natie Swirsky was a decidedly 'iffy' sort of fellow. Gus Trupshaw said, 'Iffy-what?'

Sally came by while I was kicking a football against the garage wall. She showed me a cardboard shoebox she'd made into a shooting gallery for her marbles which she carried in a white tobacco bag with a draw-string neck. She'd cut small doorways into the side of the box. Each doorway had a number written above it, ranging from 1 to 20. I lost seventeen marbles in a row before she said she was bored. I told her about the Cairo cathouse in Swirsky's pharmacy. Sally drew the strings of her bag tight and put the bag in the shoebox.

'If we go down there, Martin, promise me you'll look at Mrs Swirsky's teeth.'

*

Swirsky had been decorating his shop window. He'd cut out pink paper letters and pasted them across the glass: *1954 The Year of Swirsky & Swirsky!* In the window he had built a pyramid of banana-shaped babies' bottles, all wearing their teats. Above the pyramid he'd hung a picture of King George and Queen Elizabeth. The King wore naval uniform. The Queen wore a big blue hat. He knew they were out of date but replacements had not reached him from across the water. Swirsky smiled. He asked Sally if she'd care to purchase some French perfume for her next trip to Paris.

Swirsky's moustache lay quietly under his nose. He smoothed its wings with his soft, round hands. First left and then right. I had the feeling that, without his pink palms to soothe it, his moustache might lift off and flap away to the sky. He bowed towards his wife who was wearing a white coat just like his.

'My better half handles perfumes and patents. Beauty is as beauty does. Please apply to her,' Swirsky said to us. 'I look after prescriptions. Welcome to the well-oiled machine. Between Ruthie and me, we're going to make Swirsky's pharmacy the best in Jo'burg.'

In her white coat Ruth Swirsky's red hair turned coppery and her green eyes seemed wider than ever. 'Do you young people like Verdi, the master of melody?'

Sally said she wasn't sure. I said nothing.

Ruthie said, 'Nathan, these children are without shoes.'

Swirsky winked at us. 'That's very South African. You see kids on the Estate going barefoot morning, noon and night. You'll soon get used to it.'

Ruthie said she hoped she would. 'It must be splendid for the toes.'

I looked at her teeth. They were long and white. You could not miss them. Like her words, big clear English words. She didn't speak her words, she gave them out. You felt those words had also been raised in Wimbledon.

Swirsky told us that Ruthie believed in the life of the mind. 'She's brought all her Wimbledon books to South Africa. Filled several trunks chock-a-block. The captain of our boat swore he'd seen nothing like it. We travelled Union Castle, of course. Big ship comfort. If ever you kids want to visit the Swirsky library, say but the word. Everything is here from *Verdi, Master of Melody*, to *The Mysteries of the Vacuum*.'

'I'm planning to introduce opera to the Badminton Estate,' said Ruth Swirsky. 'I do hope you'll come.'

I said I would. Sally just looked at her feet. Then she licked her finger, leaned down and cleaned the red dust from between her toes. Then she licked her finger again. Sometimes the red dust covered the street signs so that the names of English kings and queens vanished.

'Won't that make you ill, dear?' Ruth Swirsky asked.

'I don't think so,' Sally smiled. 'I'm used to it. Aren't you used to it, Mart?'

And because I was her friend, I said, 'Yes. We're all used to it.'

We heard often how Mr and Mrs Swirsky sailed back to South Africa on the Union Castle Line. Swirsky told everybody how there was nothing to beat 'Big Ship Comfort'. The Swirskys had tried living in Cape Town, to begin with. But Ruthie had not taken to Cape Town. Then they had travelled to Durban and stayed at the New Butterworth Hotel.

'If I hear another word about the Magnolia Room and Roof Garden, or how you can tune in to the Orchid Orchestra from your luxurious bedroom in the New Butterworth Hotel, I think I'll scream,' said my mother.

'The Swirskys also had the Hammond Organ piped into their room,' my father said.

'If the New Butterworth Hotel really is the cat's pyjamas why didn't he stay there?' My mother dipped her chin and raised her eyebrows. 'Between you, me and the gatepost, Gordon, I think Nathan Swirsky might have gone out on a limb. One minute he's swanning around the globe. Next thing he's married to someone he's known for barely two minutes. And now she's walking around wearing one of his coats – what next?'

My father was leaning on his shovel and wiping sweat from his forehead when Swirsky arrived. He was wearing a pale green safari suit and yellow sandals. His calves were meaty and spiked with strong black hairs.

'It's hotter being home than it was at Tobruk,' my father said. 'Tell me how it is that South Africa can be hotter than the deserts of North Africa?'

'I was very impressed with London,' said Swirsky. 'Give it a buzz some time.'

My father shook his head. 'It took me years to get this rockery into shape. Before I go anywhere, I'm going to get my Mexican sunflowers to stand up for themselves – if it kills me.'

'Your Mexican sunflower likes a sunny place with loose, friable soil,' Swirsky said.

'They're also supposed to get on in dry places with a poor soil,' said my father sadly, kicking the stems of the sunflowers with his Army boot. 'But you try telling that to these no-good bonzos. Yes sirree.'

'Soldier's reward,' Swirsky said. Even though he had been a pilot in the Air Force.

Our fathers were always talking of the soldier's reward. No one rememered it was nine years since the War had ended and they had been demobbed and came home to Civvie Street. They missed the War and spoke of the battles in the western deserts 'Up North' as if everything had been good then. 'It was no picnic, Martin,' my father would say to me from time to time. But it seemed to have been a picnic. All our fathers knew someone who had not come home from North Africa. But somehow it still seemed a picnic. When they felt they were really living. In Tobruk, El Alamein and Alexandria it had been picnics all the way. Everything had been possible then. Even Mexican sunflowers would have bloomed in the desert, yes sirree!

'Time to wet your whistle, Natie?' my father asked, throwing down his shovel.

'Lead on, Macduff,' said Swirsky. 'Show us the way, Martin, and I'll buy you an orange squash.'

'That's very white of you, Natie,' said my father.

'Martin and I are old friends,' said Swirsky. 'Martin's going to be making use of the Swirsky library. Aren't you boy? He told Ruthie he'd also come to her opera, when she gives it. Operetta's not grand enough for my Ruthie. She wants the real thing. She thinks Badminton is ready for it now.'

'Strewth, Natie,' my father's eyes widened. 'You mean women with large chests and blokes in tights?'

Swirsky patted his moustache as we walked along the sanitary lane to the Club. 'Abso-bloody-lutely, Gordon. The full catastrophe. Ruthie loves it. Opera and Ruthie are like that.' He pressed two fingers together.

My father and Gus Trupshaw had founded the ex-servicemen's club in a corner of the kindergarten hall. In the evenings the club always smelt of Plasticine and flour-and-water glue which the kids used during the day. In the mornings it always smelt of old beer and bottletops. My father unlocked the pantry where the bottles were kept. He gave me an orange squash and soda water in a paper cup. Then he poured two beers.

'Here's to those who like us. And to hell with those who don't,' Swirsky raised his glass.

'Toodle-oo,' said my father.

I sat under a plastic palmtree at a table covered with a paper cloth. *Provided by Courtesy of Viceroy Cigarettes.* There was a picture of a man in a dinner jacket lighting cigarettes for two women who wore long white gloves. The man was tall and slim and he wore a white scarf around his neck. His hair was dark and long and sleek. I began memorizing the message written below the picture of the smokers:

> *The man who maintains that Viceroy is the finest cigarette money can buy always places himself in a strong position. Firstly, because the only judge of a cigarette is the man who smokes it. Secondly, because the weight of opinion is always on his side.*

My father wandered over and looked at the man lighting the cigarettes of the two women. 'Know that type. Probably a gent's outfitter in Civvie Street before the War. Typical lounge lizard. We got them up in Alex. Always after the Waafs.'

Swirsky patted his own smooth dark hair and said: 'It's the continental look.'

'After the Waafs for what,' I asked.

'A bit of slap and tickle,' said Swirsky.

'Never mind, Martin. The Waafs have gone the way of all good things.' My father fetched another couple of beers. 'Time for the other half, Natie?'

'Just a quick one,' said Swirsky. 'Ruthie's minding the shop.'

'Confined to barracks,' said my father and lifted his glass. 'Never thought I'd see you in matrimonial bliss, Natie. But I suppose it comes to the best of us. Chin, chin.'

Swirsky drained his beer and wiped foam from his moustache with the collar of his safari suit. 'Ruthie's taking time to settle in. She finds Africa a bit slow. Can't say I blame her. Wimbledon was all go. Let's say that she's feeling her way. I've taken on some household help. Her name's Sunny. Sunny has taken to the pharmacy like a duck to water. And Ruthie loves her. Ruthie says that she and Sunny are going to be terrific chums.'

My father raised his eyebrows in an 'if-you-say-so-Natie' way and took a swallow of his beer. 'Right-ho,' he said.

When we got home I said to my mother, 'What's a Waaf?'

She was in the bedroom, sitting in front of the mirror giving herself a home perm. Her dark hair was pulled tightly around the curlers and they stuck out like little white bones all over her head. The room smelt of boiling bones. She had a curler in her mouth.

My father rested his chin on her shoulder with his cheek next to hers and stared at their two faces in the mirror: 'Which twin has the Toni?'

With the curler between her teeth my mother said, 'I hope you haven't been putting ideas into the boy's head? What the Waafs got up to in wartime Alexandria is not for Martin or I to know, thank you very much.'

'Talking of girls, the Swirskys have taken on a domestic,' my father said. 'Nathan tells me that she and Ruth are great chums.'

The curler fell from my mother's mouth.

I said, 'She's called Sunny.'

My mother picked up the curler she'd dropped and twisted her hair around it so tightly that my scalp tingled.

'Thank you, Martin. When I wish to know what Ruth Swirsky calls her servants, I'll ask. Where on earth does she think she is? What will the other servants make of it? Will we all have to be chums? That sort of thing may be fine in Wimbledon. I dare say they do it all the time in the New Butterworth Hotel. But this is Badminton and we have troubles enough. I'm not blaming Ruth. She's from England. But I'd have thought her husband would put his foot down.'

'Monica,' said my father quietly, 'Natie's only just married the woman. He's dotty about her.'

'That,' said my mother, 'is no excuse. Look at what happened to Margot van Reen when she got too friendly with certain persons who shall be nameless. She had a little dilemma, didn't she? Well, that might be fine and dandy for Margot van Reen. But what about the rest of us? We're the ones who suffer.'

My mother had never forgotten how Swirsky took off in his car for Cape Town and left us to cope with Margot van Reen's little dilemma.

Later that afternoon as Tony and I were walking in Elizabeth Crescent we met Mrs van Reen and golden Anastasia out for a stroll. The baby sat in a pushchair and her mother said to her, 'Say hello to these handsome esquires.' Anastasia smiled and showed her gums. Tony and I felt a little bit embarrassed to be called 'esquires'. It wasn't a word that belonged to us. Or to anyone we knew. It was one of those words you only got in books.

Around the corner we bumped into Sally. She was standing barefoot on the sandy street, balanced on two empty coffee cans. She had threaded loops of string through the cans and was using them as stubby, silver stilts. She had on this tight lemon dress. She wore her hair long and loose now. She pushed a bit into her mouth and chewed it. Pulling on the string loops, and sticking out her legs so stiffly her knees turned white, she stamped down Charles Drive on the shining coffee cans singing, 'Excuse me, Mr Ex-quire . . . Don't mention it, Mrs Sire!'

'If you must know,' said her brother, 'the word is *Esquire*.'

Sally stepped off her stilts and slung them over her shoulder like tin fish. The sunshine burned in her hair until it turned buttery. She said to me, 'It's terrible to live in a world where your brother knows everything in the world? Hey, Mart?'

Tony said: 'Martin hasn't got a brother.'

'See what I mean?' his sister sighed. She reached behind her and scratched the back of her right knee. I could feel the heat in her hair. There was red sand between her toes. Her brown legs began curving from behind her knees in a line that went down to her ankles. Looking at the line I felt hungry.

'Do you see what I see?' Sally asked.

Two women in white coats were walking towards us down Henry Street. They were both wearing high-heeled shoes. Ruthie Swirsky was talking in her clear up and down English voice to a tall, round black woman who wore a yellow hat. Ruthie had stuck her arm through the arm of the woman. When they got closer we saw that the woman also wore large gold earrings. Sometimes the sun shone on Ruthie's white teeth. Sometimes it flashed on the golden earrings. Watching them you felt they had a third invisible person with them. And the invisible person was deaf. So Ruthie spoke her clear English and her friend turned it into sign-language. When Ruthie talked the black woman waved her long fingers at the deaf person we could not see.

They turned the corner into Edward Avenue and stood beneath the bluegums where the burglars were said to hide. Ruth spoke so clearly we could hear her half a block away. She said, 'Some English people don't, but I respect Winston Churchill. Did you know he spent time in South Africa. Just like me. Isn't that amazing?'

And the long black fingers of the other woman waved like ferns, saying, right back, that this was absolutely amazing.

'That must be Sunny,' I said.

'Why are they doing that?' Sally asked.

'Mrs Swirsky's talking and Sunny is showing that she's listening.'

'But why?'

'Because they're chums.'

'Chums?' Sally shivered. Then she said, 'Gosh!'

After about a week, everyone had seen them walking around the Estate. My mother said to my father, 'Gordon, you'll have to do something.'

'Perhaps you'd like to report the matter to the police? Then the government will pass a law banning the wearing of white coats,' said my father.

'Nathan Swirsky's a qualified pharmacist,' my mother said. 'So he can wear a white coat. He earned it. But his wife sells soap. It's the giddy limit.'

'This bloody government has banned mixed marriages. And communists. And films. I'm sure they're just dying to ban white coats. I'll nip along and have a word to them, Monica,' my father said.

'Even if, for argument's sake, Ruthie was entitled to one,' said my mother, 'that's no reason for giving one to the serving girl. And then walking around the Estate in broad daylight, together. Just thinking about it gives me the heeby-jeebies.'

My father went along to Swirsky's pharmacy and came home and told us he could not get a word in edgeways. Mrs Raubenheimer was there telling Swirsky that the staff at the Home were becoming uppity.

Swirsky asked what she meant by uppity and Mrs Raubenheimer had said, 'They're chancing their arms. And we all know *why* they're chancing their arms, Mr Swirsky.'

All Swirsky had said was, 'Do we?'

And Mrs Raubenheimer had shot back, 'Yes, we do, Mr Swirsky. They're all asking for white coats next.'

My mother said, 'I wouldn't normally go in to bat for Mrs Raubenheimer and her crowd. They're usually pretty good at getting their own way. But this time I support her one hundred per cent.'

I said, 'The weight of opinion is always on your side.'

'Why, thank you, Martin.' My mother looked pleased.

'He gets that stuff from the Viceroy ads down at the Club,' said my father.

'I don't care if he gets it from the Emperor of China,' said my mother.

We were walking past Eric's place and saw him being chased around the garden by his leathery, puffing mother. Eric sometimes said that she even had muscles in her neck. Eric's ma was holding a box of Goldflake Fifties in each hand and she was yelling, 'I'll give you double-storeys, young man!' As she chased Eric across the lawn, cigarettes spilled from the boxes as she beat him and she left a trail of filter-tips lying in the grass like skinny mushrooms.

'Goldflake cigarettes are the men's cigarettes women like,' said Tony as we watched Eric's ma slapping his ears with her Goldflake boxes.

'Does it hurt your head, knowing so much?' Sally asked.

When his ma gave up and went inside Eric came over to us. His cheeks were burning red and one eye was almost closed. He said, 'My head's singing.' The houses he had been building, using bits of builder's scrap, were getting bigger. He'd built a mansion with two storeys so that maybe his dead brother Sammie would want to come back and live in it. Sammie liked big houses, said

Eric. And he'd taken a few cans of condensed milk and sardines from his ma's pantry. Sammie was bound to be hungry having been away so long. When his ma found she was missing groceries, she went inside and fetched her two boxes of Goldflake Fifties.

We took Eric to see Swirsky who examined his swollen face and said, 'You might have suffered a perforated ear-drum.'

Eric looked pleased. He was always happy when something threatened his life. We knew he really wanted to be dead so that he could see Sammie again. But he never got dying right.

Swirsky plugged Eric's ears with cottonwool. He stepped out on to the pavement with us and took from the pocket of his white coat a couple of pink cards covered with purple writing. 'Badminton Ball. Bar. Buffet. Dancing to the music of the Jerry Oppenheimer Trio. Ten shillings per couple. All proceeds in aid of the South African National Tuberculosis Association.'

Swirsky put his thumbs behind his lapels and bent them like cardboard. 'May we count on your presence on Saturday night?' His black hair was combed straight back ever since he'd been to England and found a wife and his parting ran through his hair, soft and shining. He patted Sally on the head. 'You look like you'd enjoy a few waltzes. Ruthie and I have waltzed in Vienna to the strains of the Blue Danube. I urge you to follow our example when you're next down that way.'

Then his wife appeared in the doorway wearing a white coat and carrying an armful of books. Swirsky said, 'Must love you and leave you, comrades, duty calls.'

Mrs Swirsky rested her soft white chin on the pile of books in her arms and said between her clenched teeth, 'I have a bone to pick with you, Nathan Swirsky.'

Swirsky winked at us and drew his finger across his throat. 'Remember me. I may not get out of this one alive.'

'If you don't, sir, would you please give my love to Sammie?' Eric called as he walked into his shop.

We went and sat down outside the Rug Doctor's. We heard Ruthie's cries from the room above the pharmacy. Then the window opened and Ruth Swirsky started throwing books out of the window. The books hit the street like shot birds, raising a little dust. It went on for quite a while and each time Ruth threw a book out of the window she called out, 'Nathan J. Swirsky!'

When the books stopped flying from the window there was silence. We wandered over and stood among the servants who had gathered. Mr Benjamin, the Rug Doctor, came out and looked at the books and said, 'Oy, yoi, yoi.' He picked up a copy of *Pharmacology for Second Year Students*, and shook his head. 'This could have killed someone.'

Among the books in the dust we found *The Story of an African Farm*. Five *Reader's Digest* condensed books. Six paperbacks by Zane Grey. A book called *The Amateur Gentleman*. A couple of *Union Castle Year Books* for 1952 and 1953. And a very heavy *Life of Cecil John Rhodes*.

Mrs Raubenheimer stopped by and picked up a copy of *Beautiful Vienna, Waltzers' Paradise*. 'I grew up in Vienna,' she said. 'Then Hitler came. It killed the waltzing.'

Swirsky came out of his shop and stood in the sunshine. He stared at the sky, as if he was expecting rain. His face was red and his moustache looked black and sharp. The maid, Sunny, was with him, in her white coat. Swirsky pointed to the books. 'Pick them up and put them back where they belong.'

Sunny took off her white coat. The books were very dusty and she didn't want to dirty her coat. Then Ruth Swirsky stepped out into the sunshine and when she saw that Sunny had taken off her coat, she took off hers too. Now only Swirsky wore a white coat.

Mrs Raubenheimer smiled and left. The crowd of servants began melting away.

'Ours was a marriage and a mingling, Nathan Swirsky,' said

Ruthie. 'I came all the way to Africa in good faith. And what do I find after we've been married barely two minutes? You've been sneaking around putting your name in all your books as if you expected a divorce tomorrow.'

We helped Sunny to gather the books and gave them to her one at a time. Sunny dusted each with her long, thin, speaking fingers and blew the red dust from their pages.

'Ours *is* a marriage and a mingling – Ruthie darling,' Swirsky cried. 'But books are better separate.'

'South Africans!' Ruthie Swirsky shook her head. 'Separations in everything. Schools, buses, churches, streets. They even separate their bloody books! Sunny, leave those books. If the master wants them collected, let the master bally well do his dirty work himself.'

Sunny slowed and stopped. She looked at Swirsky, then at Ruth. Then she went on picking up the books.

'Sunny knows that master must be obeyed.' Ruthie shook her head again so that her red hair shone in the sunshine. 'Poor little sod.' She walked into the shop.

'Sunny knows who pays her wages,' said Swirsky.

Eric wandered over carrying a book called *Voices from the Other Side*. 'May I borrow this, Mr Swirsky?'

'Be my guest, boykie,' said Swirsky. 'Another good read, courtesy of Swirsky's flying library.'

On Wednesday Mr Govender, the vegetable seller, arrived as usual in his rackety van with the green tarpaulin stretched across bamboo poles. We ran after Mr Govender's truck shouting, 'Sammy, Sammy, what you got? Missus, Missus, apricot. Some is good and some is not . . .'

Ruthie Swirsky walked down Henry Street in high heels and a big straw hat. Sunny walked behind her carrying a big basket. She did not wear her yellow hat. Or her gold earrings. Or her white coat. And her thin fingers said nothing. Ruth Swirsky said loudly: 'Good afternoon, Mr Greengrocer. What do you have today?'

Mr Govender pushed his head through the curtain of flat paperbags spiked on hooks, and brown as smoked kippers, strung along the bamboo poles, and stared at her.

'Avocados look as green as grass,' said Ruthie Swirsky and her voice rang clear in the street. She bought pears, peaches, apricots and handed them to Sunny. When Sunny's basket was full, she handed her a whole box of tomatoes. Sunny balanced the box of tomatoes on her head and walked home behind Ruth Swirsky.

'I really think Ruthie's getting the feel of things,' said my mother.

Next day Sally, Tony and I were walking along Edward Avenue where the bluegums lined the little river. We saw Eric, sitting on the branch of a tree, reading *Voices from the Other Side*.

Eric saw us and he said, 'Hey, I think I'm psychic.'

Sally said, 'You're mad. You poor mutt.'

She was wearing a white blouse with pearly buttons and blue shorts. There was mud on her knees. She looked at me and said, 'Will you be my chum?'

Tony picked up a flat stone and skipped it along the iron-hard road until it hit a telephone pole and died with a clang.

More than anything I wanted to say yes.

Tony dusted his hands on his khaki shorts. 'You can't be,' he said. 'Not here.'

'Who says?' his sister asked. 'Martin can be whatever he wants, can't you, Mart?'

Nobody said anything. But I knew Tony had got hold of

something. Some words were not for us. They only worked in England, perhaps. Where they were in a strong position. It was something heavy Tony had got hold of. Like the weight of opinion. And it wasn't on our side.

LOVE SONGS

RUTHIE Swirsky began wearing her dirndl.

She went walking up and down Henry Street. Puffy sleeves and fat daisies embroidered on her padded shoulders, and her big green dress swinging at her ankles. She looked tough and strange. Whenever she met someone from the Jewish Old Age Home she would begin singing very loudly, in German. And Dr Moishe or Mrs Raubenheimer would tighten their lips and hurry on home.

We knew the songs she sang. They came from *The Merry Widow.*

Gus Trupshaw said, 'She reminds me of the Lady in White who used to sing the troop ships out to sea. Except for that very rummy frock she wears.'

'It's called a dirndl,' said my father.

'You're pulling my leg, Gordon. That sounds the sort of thing you only get in rubber goods shops.'

'Natie told me,' said my father. 'It's Austrian national costume. Or some such bloody nonsense.'

'Fair enough,' said Gus Trupshaw. 'But why the Jerry outfit?'

'I asked him that. He got that look he always gets when he talks about her. Seems Ruthie's gunning for Raubenheimer, *et al.* The Jewish Old Age Home tried to close down her show.

Remember? They said there were rather too many Huns for harmony in Ruthie's production of *The Merry Widow.* And she hasn't forgotten it. Or as Natie puts it – Ruthie remembers.'

The week before Christmas and the sun had baked our roads to a cracked, dry, biscuit brown. They were too hot to walk on barefoot after eleven in the morning. There was a spate of burglaries in Edward Avenue. My mother said the servants were just taking their Christmas boxes early. If people gave their servants the run of the place, what could they expect?

Our fathers began mounting special night-time patrols along Edward Avenue. Along the line of tall, thick bluegums that grew beside the little stream. Our fathers carried torches, sticks and their old Army-issue pistols. But they found no burglars. What they found, or rather heard, was the sound of a man weeping in the bluegums.

Gus Trupshaw had called on him to advance slowly with his hands in the air or face the consequences. My father dropped to one knee and offered to cover Gus Trupshaw with his Browning. But Gus Trupshaw said he'd rather not. Everyone knew that my father had been in the Pay Corps.

Eric's father told us all this as we sat in our kitchen. His gun had jammed. He was supposed to be on his way to call the police. My mother said we'd had quite enough of police around Badminton. If three grown men couldn't deal with someone crying in the bluegums without sending for the police then she was very sorry for them.

My father and Gus Trupshaw arrived next and sat down looking a bit foolish. Where was the prisoner, my mother asked.

'We took no prisoners,' said Gus Trupshaw.

'It was Swirsky, in the bluegums,' said my father.

'Crying in the bluegums?' asked my mother. 'Alone?'

'So we left him there.' Trupshaw looked embarrassed. 'After

all, if that's his idea of a good night out, well, it's a free country.'

'I'm not so sure about that,' said my father. 'Since this damn government of dyed-in-the-wool fascists came in, in '48, it's been like living in a bloody great prisoner-of-war camp. Sometimes I think I prefer Jerry to this lot.'

'I definitely prefer Jerry to this lot,' said Gus Trupshaw.

My father ate his cheese sandwich and sipped his coffee. Eric's father said he had better be getting back to the missus and, no, he would not have a cheese sandwich. Cheese made him dream.

'Lucky bugger,' said Gus Trupshaw.

And my mother said, 'Can we watch our language?'

'Swirsky was wearing his white coat,' said my father, 'and he was carrying a book called *Verdi, Master of Melody*. Can't bloody well think why. It was too damn dark for him to read. And he was bawling his head off.'

My mother sighed. 'It always gets this way towards Christmas time. So much for the season of good will.'

Tony and I were on a patch of waste ground behind the Greek Tea Room when Swirsky came by and stopped to watch us having a top fight. We'd roll our chunky wooden tops, with their bright steel points, in waxy yellow twine and then we'd try to peg each other's top. Swirsky knelt by the fighting circle and watched as Tony's blue pegged my red, took a chunk out of the wood but did not split it.

'The clash of the Titans,' said Swirsky. 'This is a game that goes back to Ancient Greece, my boys. When you next visit Greece don't miss the Oracle at Delphi. And when you meet a Greek, say to him, "*Kalimera, filo.*" It means "Good morning, my friend".'

His pink face was soft and rumpled. His eyes looked bruised.

Swirsky usually fitted his chemist's coat like a fat letter in a fine white envelope. Now his white coat looked like he'd slept in it. And he hadn't shaved. There was stubble all over his chin and amongst the strong black hairs, here and there, was a thin wiry white hair. But worst of all was his moustache. It hung from his lips in the way of not very well pegged washing on the line. And instead of being black and sharp when the light caught it, it seemed the colour of rather weak tea.

From amongst the ballpoint pens in his top pocket he took three twists of barley-sugar and gave a piece each to Tony and me. We didn't know what to say or do. I caught Tony's look. You gave barley-sugar to babies. Still, we liked Swirsky, so we ate our barley-sugar. Swirsky felt like a rain cloud. He made you want to head indoors before the heavens opened. Swirsky had never made us want to run away before. We went on pegging tops, sucking our barley-sugar twists, while Swirsky watched, saying nothing.

I hit Tony's top dead centre and split it clean down the middle. It lay on the ground like the halves of a perfect peach. The wood grain ran in parallel ridges, blond alternating with caramel. Swirsky reached down and picked up the two halves of Tony's top. He held them in his palms for a moment and then he pressed them hard together. Then he dropped both halves back into the circle.

'One dead top,' said Swirsky. He walked off and he didn't look back.

Soon after that we heard that the Jewish Old Age Home had withdrawn all its business from Swirsky's pharmacy. They were using Lipschitz in Orange Grove, even though that meant a trip of several miles because Lipschitz didn't deliver.

'I can't say I blame them,' said my mother. 'Mrs Raubenheimer doesn't need me on her side, you can be sure of that. But

I know just how she feels. Every time she sets foot out of her front door there is Ruthie in full cry. Singing German songs at the top of her voice. You don't have to be Jewish to find that a bit much. I know I wouldn't like it. And that funny floral dress she wears. What does she think she looks like?'

One morning as we were walking past Swirsky's pharmacy we saw him sitting on the sidewalk outside his shop wearing his white coat and reading *Verdi, Master of Melody*. From the room above the shop we heard the sounds of someone singing in German. A grey Volkswagen minibus was parked across the road. Because it was so hot, Swirsky was wearing khaki shorts under his white coat and his knees were round and pink. They looked like hot moons.

'Welcome to Salzburg. Will you join me in a glass of beer or Schnapps?'

He went into the shop and came out with a jug of barley water and three glasses. He also had a tube of Kolynos toothpaste. He invited us to taste the chlorophyll in the toothpaste because he said it healed faster than penicillin. Then he poured us each a glass of barley water.

'I drink to your eyes, young lady,' he said to Sally.

I lifted my glass and said, 'Your very good health, sir.' That was what the man did in the Castle lager ads printed on the paper tablecloths down at the ex-servicemen's club.

Swirsky said, 'By Heavens. I do believe I have just been toasted by Raymond Glendenning, world-famous BBC commentator.'

'Is Mrs Swirsky learning to sing?' Tony asked.

'Mrs Swirsky knows how to sing,' said Swirsky. 'But she's improving her technique. Mrs Swirsky has a cultural side. So she is putting herself in the hands of a maestro and practising her opera. Mrs Swirsky visited the opera once a month when she

171

lived in Wimbledon. South Africa must seem a long way from anywhere, when you've spent your life in Wimbledon. Opera puts Ruthie in touch with Europe. Ruthie needs to be in touch with Europe, or she will wither.'

I sat there and tried to imagine what that meant. How would Ruthie wither? Would her skin shrink like a sprig of lavender, growing grey and cold? Would her red hair pale like a rose petal pressed between the pages of a book? Would her white arms and legs dry to a cinder like the peachadilla creeper after our fathers tore it down when they chased Nicodemus from the roof of Margot van Reen's summer house? Above our heads Ruthie's voice climbed a series of steps, as if it were going up a very tall staircase and then, just as carefully, climbed down again.

Early that evening I was in Victoria Road where I had been improving my catapult technique shooting at street poles until Gus Trupshaw came by and told me to stop because a catapult was a lethal weapon. As I was walking home the grey minivan raced past me kicking up gravel, stinging my legs. Ruth Swirsky was sitting close to the blond German singer who had kissed her hand after the second and final performance of *The Merry Widow.* She was licking an ice-cream cone.

When the sun went down something strange happened. I lay in bed, wondering how Ruthie would wither? Wondering how chlorophyll in toothpaste worked faster than penicillin? In the back yards the dogs, Adolf and Attila and Genghis, had been barking like mad, as they always did after dark, warning the burglars with their fishing rods that they were in for a nasty surprise. Then the singing started and the dogs fell quiet. The rise and fall of my mother and father's voices from the front room stopped suddenly. They listened. The dogs listened. Through the darkness we could hear a man singing 'The Tennessee Waltz'. I heard the front door open and my mother and father walked out into the garden.

They came indoors when the singing stopped and I heard my father say, 'That takes the giddy biscuit.'

After that we heard the phantom singer every night. He liked 'The Tennessee Waltz' because he sung it three times. But he also sang the big Johnny Ray number, 'Cry!'. And 'How Much Is That Doggie In The Window?' and 'High Noon'.

No one mentioned the secret night-time singer. Just as we said nothing about the arrival and departure of the night-soil men who came with their horse and cart after dark and carried away the black buckets that stood in the sanitary lanes outside each house. Just as we said nothing about Maggie who took off her clothes from time to time and tore around her house while her father chased her with a blanket.

But after the secret singer's concert each evening, my parents, who thought I was asleep, talked about the mystery. 'Little Tommy Tucker's singing for his supper,' my father would say.

'I really don't understand how people can do that sort of thing, Gordon. What must the other shopkeepers think? What do they feel across the road when this starts up?'

'Across the road' was my mother's way of referring to the Jewish Old Age Home. I pictured her, rolling her *Women's Weekly* magazine into a truncheon as she spoke. Her eyes wide, shaking her head at my father as she asked these questions and showing her hands with open palms, the way she always did when she was flabbergasted.

'I met Mrs Raubenheimer in Alexandra Road today. She was talking to Margot van Reen. Everyone's been talking to Margot since the singing started. It's drawn people together. And Mrs Raubenheimer said, "Johnny Ray, he's not." No more than that. But Margot van Reen and I knew instantly who she was referring to.'

My father said, 'A couple of us went around there the other night. He stands out in the back yard. You know where they have that loquat tree? That's where he stands out in the back yard, and directs his songs at her window.'

'She must know he's doing it,' said my mother.

'You can hear him miles away,' said my father. 'And when he sings "Jezebel", he gives it all he's got. But how his love songs are received, I really couldn't say. There's a light on in her window. But the place is as silent as the grave. I don't fancy his chances of supper – little Tommy Tucker.'

'Why is there always trouble at Christmas?' My mother's voice rose high and shaky. 'Didn't I say that, Gordon? What must the servants think? They're listening to this like everybody else. What goes through their little minds? And next time they get drunk and start banging on the street poles and I ask them to stop, they're going to turn to me and say, "How can you say that? When one of your lot has been crying for the moon like a lovelorn spaniel for the past week?" And I can't say I blame them. Oh, Gordon, I won't know where to put my face.'

After about a week the singing stopped. The nights were filled again with the whistles of burglar alarms. Or the barking of the big dogs in our back yards. Or the occasional sounds of shots as some father ran out into the night and began blasting away with his service pistol. But the singer was quiet.

My mother was relieved. 'Thank Heavens, things are back to normal. My nerves were worn to a frazzle.'

Swirsky came by the next morning, when my father was planting out some strelitzias.

'The strelitzia loves a bit of shattered brick and lots of well-rotted manure,' he told Swirsky.

'It's amazing what creatures love,' said Swirsky. 'Read this, Gordon.'

He gave my father a piece of paper.

My father read it out.

Dear Natie

Wolfgang and I have gone to New York. Please try to understand.
Your motorbike will be waiting for you at the airport. Remember,
God is love.

                                                                    Love, Ruthie

My father folded the note and handed it back to Swirsky.

'They borrowed my motorbike, Gordon. I wondered why
they didn't take the Volkswagen mini-bus. But I suppose that that
belongs to the operatic troupe. So they borrowed my bike instead.
To get to the airport.'

My father threw down his small sharp gardening spade
and it stuck in the lawn, quivering. 'Well, I'll be buggered!' he
said.

'The thing is, they didn't get to the airport. They had a
puncture and must have hitched the rest of the way. My bike's
standing out on the airport road and I need a bit of help to get it
back. It's my delivery vehicle, you know. Might I prevail upon
you, Gordon?'

'Did they just up and scarper?' my father asked. 'Ruthie and
the singing Hun?'

Swirsky said, 'It's 6,087 miles to New York from Johannesburg, as the crow flies.'

Our fathers went to fetch Swirsky's motorbike from the place it
had been ditched on the road to the airport. They mounted it on
the back of Gus Trupshaw's new Ford truck and he drove very
slowly down Henry Street.

Everyone came out to watch, though my mother said, 'The
servants won't do a stroke of work, after this.'

Eric, who knew about these things, because he was reading Sammie's books, said it was like watching the Romans returning in triumph from some mighty battle, bearing the spoils of war.

And Sally got rather carried away and shouted out, 'Bravo!'

The Harley Davidson stood in Swirsky's back yard under the loquat tree. It stood there darkly for days and days, left alone as if it were radioactive. Black and dangerous under the tree. We used to go and look at it every day. We looked and we looked but we still couldn't believe it.

Eric stopped turning builder's rubble into houses that fell down and, instead, he began building tree houses. Platforms of planks, higher and higher, in the branches of the tallest trees he could find.

Ruthie had done something really amazing. Bigger and better than anything anyone we knew had ever done before. It made us giddy. Tony and Sally and Eric and I got out an atlas. We stared at the great stretch of ocean between Africa and America, and we felt even giddier.

'You pay 7/6 for a Coke in America,' Tony said.

My mother said to my father, 'Well, I'm sorry to say that I'm not surprised. If you make your bed, you have to lie in it. Fill your head with dreams of foreign places all day long and you mustn't be surprised if people believe they can just get up and go there, any time they wish.'

The people from the Jewish Old Age Home were in and out of Swirsky's pharmacy all day long after that. They took away their business from Lipschitz in Orange Grove. But they had to go and fetch their medicines themselves because Swirsky wasn't delivering any more.

My mother said, 'I must say I take my hat off to them – the way they support their own. They're very good that way.'

We waited and we watched. Swirsky's big Harley Davidson

stood beneath the loquat tree, all alone. We still couldn't believe that anyone had moved as far away as Ruthie. Swirsky had gone as far as London. My mother said they paid nineteen and six in the pound in income tax, in England. But Ruthie had gone all the way to America.

Swirsky had said in ten years' time Cape Town would be another New York. Ruthie hadn't been ready to wait to see what happened to Cape Town. We longed for Swirsky to kick his Harley Davidson into life again. To put on his leather flying helmet, jump on the great big bike with its big wide petrol tank and its twirly handlebars, as if he were riding some huge black bull, and go flying down Henry Street. But he never did. And we went on waiting and watching, until we couldn't bear it any more. Sally, Tony and I climbed the fence one night, crossed Swirsky's yard and we touched the cold saddle of the motorbike. We had to do that. It was the only way we could believe it. We touched it for luck. Because someone who had sat on that saddle had gone to New York.

ALOFT

O N Sunday morning Sally came flying round to my place, stood on one leg at the kitchen door and kicked off her shoes. She lifted the toes of one leg to her knee. It was only about nine but the sun was high and hot in the heavens.

'Swirsky's in the water,' said Sally. 'Standing in the dam. Right up to his waist. But he's wearing his chemist's coat. And his green tie.'

Tony wandered up behind her. Although it was baking hot, Tony wore an electric-blue sweater with one sleeve unravelling. He'd tied the loose piece of wool to his wrist.

'Why are you standing with your foot up like that? Like you were a flamingo or something?'

'You're sweating,' said Sally. 'At least flamingoes don't sweat.'

We went to find Eric so he could also see Swirsky in the water. Badminton estate had that vacant look to it which Sundays and holidays brought on. You felt everyone had gone to sleep for ever. The only movement, here and there, came from a solitary father, in his old, bleached Air Force cap or his flaking Army belt, perhaps a handkerchief covering his neck, out in his garden propagating some cacti or repotting a few plants, or cursing his strelitzias.

Eric was up in Heaven. That's what he called his treehouse

which he'd built thirty feet up a big jacaranda. 'I'm just going up to Heaven,' he'd say. And he'd pull his rope ladder up after him.

'Swirsky's standing in the dam,' Sally shouted up to Eric in . Heaven.

We ran across the veld to the dam. My father was there, his hands on his hips, whistling in a tuneless way and every so often calling to Swirsky, then looking away and whistling again as if he had just happened to be passing and might walk away at any minute if anyone else came by.

Swirsky was standing in the water up to his waist. He'd painted a big blue Star of David on the back of his white coat. A line of Black Zionists stretched into the water and Swirsky was dunking them like a machine. The rest of the members of the Church of Black Zion sat on the bank and watched.

'Come out of there, Natie,' my father spoke out of the side of his mouth. And studied the clouds overhead, pretending it all had nothing to do with him.

'My people need me,' said Swirsky and he didn't stop for a moment. 'God comes among his people. Doesn't he? Otherwise he's not much good – is he, Gordon?' And he dunked another Zionist.

'You're not even a Christian. You don't need to do that.'

'Bravo,' shouted the Zionists on the bank – in exactly the voice Ruthie Swirsky had used to cheer the singers in *The Merry Widow.*

Gus Trupshaw arrived in his new Ford. 'Shall I get a ladder? We could hold it out to him and then pull him in.'

'That's for someone who has fallen through the ice,' my father said. 'He can bloody well walk out of there, easy as winking. If he wants to.'

'What's he saying to them?' Gus Trupshaw wanted to know. 'You're supposed to say – "I baptize thee in the name of the Father and of the Son and of the Holy Ghost".'

'I don't think he's saying that,' said my father.

Swirsky wasn't saying that. He was saying, 'It's 6,008 miles from Cape Town to New York, as the boat plies.'

'I don't think you're playing the game, Natie,' my father called.

But his voice was drowned by the Church of Zion sitting on the bank of the dam who began singing 'God Bless Africa'.

Swirsky led the newly baptized in a long dripping line back to his shop. He gave away his tins of babyfood and little sachets of shampoo. I remember the bottles of chicken puree for one-year-olds were very popular. Swirsky had built a new wall across his shop from empty magnesia bottles. It was strong, three bottles deep, six foot high, stretching from nappy pins to baby food. Now he gave away the magnesia wall bottle by bottle. Then he stood at the door of his chemist's shop and watched the newly baptized leave, lifting both hands and showing open palms to the black people and then touching his palms to his chest. It was a cross between blessing them and waving goodbye.

Swirsky's baptisms caused a lot of trouble. 'The point,' said my mother, 'is that Mr Swirsky has suffered a personal loss. Why does that lead him to consort with natives? What happens if the police come around, asking questions? I don't even know if you're allowed to give away your worldly goods and chattels.'

'It's hardly likely to be against the law, Monica, giving away what you own,' said my father. 'Unless of course this bloody government has passed another law. It's bloody marvellous, isn't it? You go off to fight for King and country in the deserts of North Africa. You fight the Germans. Then you come home to find that the country's being run by men who've spent the war lighting candles for Hitler!'

'Think what these free gifts will do by the time we get to

Christmas,' said my mother. 'Every native on the estate will be at the back door demanding Christmas boxes. And they won't exactly die with gratitude when I give them a pair of my old shoes and a couple of bob. Really, Nathan Swirsky has done enough damage as it is. Look at poor little Anastasia.'

My mother thought it was Swirsky's fault that Margot van Reen had fallen in love with her gardener, Nicodemus. I remembered how the men had surrounded Nicodemus on the roof of Margot van Reen's summerhouse. How they had torn down the trellis and trampled the sweet peas and the peachadilla. How Nicodemus had sat on the summerhouse roof, with his woolly white Father Christmas beard hooked on behind his ears, while the torches played on him until our fathers pulled him down and threw a blanket over his head and we never saw him again.

What my mother called Margot van Reen's little dilemma was now a couple of years old and her mother took her walking in a push-chair, down Edward Avenue, dressed in blue and white which made the baby's skin seem even darker. Dodging the dried muddy ruts of Edward Avenue, Margot van Reen always seemed very happy when she saw us. 'Anastasia, say good afternoon to the gentlemen.' And Anastasia would smile her wide pink smile and Tony, Sally, Eric and I felt very strange to be called gentlemen.

It was about this time that the government passed a law saying that white men and black women who had brown babies could all be put in jail.

'I don't believe it,' said Tony.

'Not believing things makes you stupid,' his sister said. 'Especially when you know they're right.'

I told my mother about hearing the big blond singer from *The Merry Widow* telling Ruthie Swirsky she was the saddest woman he had ever seen.

'You don't want to go listening too closely to what grown-ups say, Martin, you could be terribly misled. Look at what happened to poor Mrs Swirsky.'

'When Swirsky left Badminton the first time he said Rhodesia was a coming little country.' My father shook his head. 'And, for Ruth, Cape Town was supposed to be like Nice. For Nathan, it was going to be another New York.'

'Which goes to prove you can't wish places into being. Only God can do that,' said my mother.

'And then, only every second Tuesday,' my father winked at me. 'At least Ruthie got to New York. I hope New York is ready for her.'

My father was out on the lawn practising his putting when Swirsky came round that Sunday morning. Without a word my father handed him a putter.

'Do you know his name? The blond one? The baritone who ran off with Ruthie?' asked Swirsky, lining up his putt.

'Can't say I do,' said my father.

'He's called Wolfgang.'

'They're all called something like that.'

'Wolfgang Christ.'

My father watched as Swirsky's ball lipped the cup. 'Too bad. Kiss and part.' My father holed his putt and gave his Bobbie Locke thumbs up. He bought a pair of plus-fours like Bobbie Locke's. Canary-yellow with blue chevrons. But he stopped wearing the gear when the servants laughed at him.

'Ruthie told me he sang like a god.'

'That's the trouble with women,' my father retrieved his ball from the cup. 'They're always fantasizing.'

'It's true, Gordon. Mrs Raubenheimer tells me it's a common German name. Even though this Christ is apparently an Austrian.

185

For all I know there are Frenchmen and Greeks called Christ. But I'll bet it's unusual in those countries. I've never come across it, I can bloody well assure you. So I get the Austrian branch of the family. Austria's probably thick with these Christs.'

'Don't let it eat you, Natie,' said my father.

'What would you say is the essence of God?'

'Hell, Natie, what a question! I just work in a bank – remember? I'm not too hot in the God department. But I'd say that, like this bloody government, God is a mystery. Well, that's what they say about him. And in a way I suppose he is. Anyone who creates Errol the topsoil man is asking for trouble. The trouble with God is that you don't get to complain, do you? You can't say, now just hold on a minute, Mr God. You can't really say anything. The essence of God? That's what you asked. Well, the essence of God, I suppose, is to be with us. But the nature of God seems to be elsewhere. And that's the trouble. He's always elsewhere. And you don't want that—do you? You don't want him always disappearing. Running off. You want him there, where you can say to him – now look Lord, or God, or Jehovah, or whatever you want to call him – stand up and be counted. Be a man.'

'Be a man,' said Swirsky. 'Yes. That's it.'

And it was later that morning that he began baptizing the Zionists in the dam.

The following day I got up at six because Eric wanted me to help him collect birds' eggs from the bluegums. As we walked down Henry Street we heard someone sobbing in Margot van Reen's summerhouse.

'It's Sammie!' Eric said and jumped the fence and ran to the trellis where the sweet-peas grew thickly and the peachadilla creeper was brilliant.

I knew it wasn't Sammie. Sammie was dead. It was Swirsky

we saw through the sweet-peas, dressed in a dark blue suit and red tie, crying his eyes out.

'What on earth is happening?' said the soft voice of Margot van Reen. She was wearing the same white silk gown she had on the night our fathers chased her servant Nicodemus from the roof of this same summerhouse. 'Oh Nathan,' she said when she saw Swirsky. 'You poor dear man!' And she put her arms around him and he rested his head on her breast.

'Will you let me save you?' asked Swirsky, his voice all muffled on account of his face being pressed to her breast.

'I've already been saved, thank you Nathan,' Mrs van Reen lifted her smoky eyes and shining hair to the early morning sun. 'I had Nicodemus – remember? He was an angel sent by God.'

'But have you even been baptized?' asked Swirsky.

About half an hour later Eric and I stood beside the dam watching Swirsky baptize Margot van Reen. She wore a peach-yellow bathing suit and a white rubber cap pulled down over her ears, which made her look like a bald angel. She held her nose and closed her eyes and Swirsky dunked her. 'God bless you, Natie,' said Margot, coming up streaming.

'Don't mention it,' said Swirsky.

He tried to baptize people all over the estate.

Sally's mother spoke for all when she said, 'Don't let me find you in that dam. Who knows what the Zionists do in there? You might get bilharzia.'

And I suppose that's what caused the trouble. Swirsky had baptized all the black Zionists. Margot van Reen let him do her. But that's where it stopped. There was no one left. None of our fathers agreed to be baptized. So Swirsky suddenly faded away. One minute he was still there, the next he was gone.

The alarms started when someone found his motorbike down by the river among the bluegums. Our fathers assembled a search party. Gus Trupshaw carried his starting pistol and they all searched the trees and the thick undergrowth along the river. We heard the men's shouts for hours.

'You over there, Gus?' my father called.

'Am proceeding in a westerly direction,' yelled Gus Trupshaw.

'Roger!' my father thundered back.

'My godfathers,' said my mother. 'Aren't men the biggest babies in the world?'

They didn't find him. Then Papas down at the Greek Tea Room said he thought that perhaps Swirsky had gone back to Rhodesia. So my father phoned the Leopard Rock Motel. 'Fishing, billiards and table tennis,' Swirsky used to say of the Leopard Rock Motel. 'A man can be king there.'

But they hadn't seen Swirsky at the Leopard Rock Motel.

'Rhodesia is the coming country,' Swirsky liked to say. 'Give it ten years and it'll be another Switzerland.'

Why was it that we always wanted what was itself to turn into somewhere else?

It was Eric who finally found him.

'I think there's someone in Heaven,' he said. 'Maybe it's Sammie, come back to life?'

It was Swirsky, in the branches of a giant tree where Eric had built the highest and most invisible of his secret places. He had pulled up the rope ladder behind him and we couldn't reach him.

'I am the living God!' he shouted from deep inside Eric's treehouse.

All the neighbours came to see for themselves.

'You come down this minute, Nathan Swirsky,' Eric's ma yelled. She lit a Goldflake and drummed her yellow fingers on the box-lid. You could see her looking around for Eric, longing to have a go at bashing his ears.

'I am a jealous God!' said Swirsky from inside the house above our heads.

Now Eric's ma was a leathery lady. Her brothers were both fast bowlers. Her dad had been a famous umpire. And she didn't take that from anyone.

She said: 'I'll give him "jealous God" all right!'

She marched straight inside and phoned the fire brigade.

They ran a ladder up to the treehouse. All the servants gathered and when Gus Trupshaw told them to go away they just laughed.

'This could be ugly,' Gus Trupshaw warned. He took out his starting pistol and fired a shot. The fire brigade arrived and pulled Swirsky out of the treehouse. He was naked, except for his moustache. And even that looked naked. Margot van Reen fetched her silk dressing-gown for him to wear because Trupshaw said the servants could not be allowed to see a white man naked. When the firemen put the dressing-gown on Swirsky my father said that the servants would be impossible to live with if they saw a white man in a lady's silk dressing-gown. The firemen brought Swirsky down the ladder.

'Put away your pistol, Gus. You'll only frighten the horses.' Swirsky gave a gentle smile at the foot of the tree.

'Did you see Sammie, sir?' Eric asked.

Swirsky put his arm around Eric's shoulders. 'Sammie says you are to stop worrying. He's fine where he is.'

Swirsky left Badminton quietly, a few days later. No one saw him go but my mother said he'd paid her a visit and recommended she go touring. When she said our Vauxhall would never get beyond Durban, he suggested that she use a deluxe motor coach of the South African Railways.

'He had the gall to say to me that they run to frequent schedules and in leisurely comfort through the Union's scenic wonderlands of mountain passes, picturesque native territories and along its rugged coastline. Can you imagine?'

No one talked of Swirsky after that. But amongst those he had baptized life was definitely better. Eric stopped building houses that fell on him and crying for his lost brother, Sammie. Little Anastasia did not get arrested under the new laws against brown babies. And the Black Zionists, gathering by the waterside, sang the song that Ruthie Swirsky had taught them: 'I get a kick out of you!'

Then a face began appearing on the blue flags under which the Zionists marched to their meetings by the dam. Tony and Eric and Sally and I recognized the moustache. Soon everyone in Badminton looked up and saw it too. Who else could it be? Swirsky might be elsewhere but he was for ever with us. Swirsky, flying aloft, high above our heads.